Cover Designer Dark Water Covers

Edited by Stephanie Alexander

NEXT AUGUST

KELLY MOORE

NEXT AUGUST SERIES BOOK ONE

NEXT August

KELLY MOORE

CHAPTER ONE

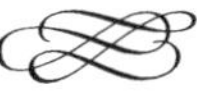

AUGUST

The view from my office always impresses me, and I'm not easily impressed. I watch the day end, another in a long line of similar workdays. Traces of orange in the sunset, balanced against the dark, metallic Seattle skyline. It's always the same, yet always different. Predictable, but just interesting enough. Sometimes it seems like that's my motto in life.

I'm on the fifteenth floor, so I can see the pedestrians scurrying out of their own offices, rushing to get home. Pike's market is shutting down for the day, no more guys flinging fish. The Ferris wheel lights up, a giant, rotating streetlamp. It's comforting to watch the city go through its routine, transitioning from day to night. I don't get up here much anymore. It's my company, but I have enough people I trust to keep an eye on things here, so I work remotely unless I have to be here. I love this city, but I don't love the stress of being around other people. I've always kept a small circle. It's easier that way.

My phone buzzes. It's my secretary. I want to ignore it, but I know Margaret won't be deterred. She'll blast through the door if I don't answer her. I swipe her name on my phone. "Yes, Margaret?"

"Mr. Rylan, did you complete the paperwork on the—"

"Yes. I just finished looking at the last scholarship recipients. Strong candidates this year."

"Yes, they are. You know this is one of my favorite projects every year. All those young nurses will do so much for so many people. It's just so nice to work on something so positive! I really liked the application of this one girl, from Sacramento—"

"Yes, I agree," I said, cutting her off. I didn't want to talk about it. While I happily provided scholarships for nursing students every year, I didn't like to think about the reason I'd started the scholarship in the first place. It was too painful. "I'll send their files over to you in the morning."

Margaret was used to my gruffness. It didn't

phase her, and she was all business again. "Yes, sir. Of course."

"Go home. It's late."

"As soon as I double check all your conference calls for next week, I will." Margaret has been working for the company for twenty-five years. She worked for my father, long before I took over operations. She's a workaholic, like me.

My phone beeps again." I told you to go home, Margaret."

"Your last appointment has arrived, sir."

I swig down a shot of bourbon and loosen my tie. I fly to this office on Mondays for two reasons. First, the board meetings. I could easily tie in via my computer from my office in Utah, but the board insists that I actually show my face. Most of them are older guys. The same age as my father. Some of them even knew him. Not that anyone talks about him anymore. He's become the family secret no one wants to talk about— even here, within his professional family. His former colleagues. So I show up, listen to the old guy's blab on and on for a couple hours, and then I do as I please anyway. No one complains. After all, I brought this company back from the brink of ruin. I'm only twenty-eight, but they trust my judgment.

The second reason is purely physical. I don't have time for relationships. I don't want the drama. And not just run of the mill drama, either. When you're one of the youngest billionaires in the United States, your drama has big potential consequences. I can't afford to have someone find out my secrets, and destroy what I've worked so hard to build. So I belong to a private club, one that connects me with women who want the same thing. No ties. Every member signs nondisclosures to protect our privacy. No commitments. Only sex.

I've been meeting Lisa every Monday night for the last three months. She's a smart, beautiful businesswoman who has dealt with her share of men who use her for their personal gain. She's been burnt one too many times, she doesn't trust easily. At this point, she and I are friends, but there's no emotional attachment between us. Sometimes we talk business, and help each other out pitching ideas, but tonight she's here for one reason, and one reason only.

Her high heels click across the polished tile floor. I mix her a dirty martini. She takes it as she sweeps past me, on her way to the door at the back of my office. It leads to a studio apartment. She unties her trench coat. She's wearing a black leather corset and nothing else, except for those sky high heels. I like the kink that she brings, but she's also a great submissive in the bedroom.

Her trench coat drops to the floor as I stride toward her. We come together, and I trace her jawline.

"August Rylan," she whispers. "It's been too long."

"It's only been a week," I reply.

She looks up at me. "A week is too long."

My fingers trail down to the curve of her breast. She inhales deeply as I release the constricting eyelets of her corset. Then I take her hand and lead her into my bedroom.

I STOP at the coffee shop on the bottom floor of the building. It's another rainy Friday morning, and the Seattle traffic will be brutal. I ended up having to spend the entire week in Seattle meeting with some potentially big clients. My limo is waiting for me out front, and the doorman escorts me with his umbrella. Fred, the driver who has carted me around for years and carted my father around before me, has the motor running.

I climb in the backseat. The leather crinkles

under me. It's a comforting smell." Good morning, Fred. How's traffic looking this morning? I want to get home."

"Brutal, as usual, sir," he says. Accident on the interstate. It's completely shut down. We'll have to take a detour, so we'll be late."

"Damn," I say. "I really want to get home."

"Don't worry, sir. I've already notified the pilot. All is well." He puts the car in drive and chuckles. "With what you pay him, he's not going anywhere."

I smile ruefully and thank him. I close the window between us and fumble for my phone in my pants pocket. He is my number one person on speed dial.

"Hey, Sam," I say, "Tell your mom I'm running late, but I will be there."

The voice on the other line is wildly enthusiastic. One thing I love about Sam—he's twenty, but he has the exuberance of a kid sometimes. Given his circumstances, that's particularly admirable. Not many people could retain such positivity after going through his trials.

"Hey, August! We're looking forward to it, man."

"Me too, dude. I'll order pizza when I get there, and Fred got us that new World at War game."

"Awesome," he says. "Since as usual, no hot date on a Friday night for me."

I cringe. "Sam—you can go on a date with anyone you want. Any girl would be—"

He laughs, and I'm reminded of the fact that even though I've taken over the big brother role for him, sometimes he seems more mature than I am. "It's okay, man. All in good time. Tonight, let's just play some World at War."

"You got it," I say, and hang up.

I push the remote that lowers the dividing window." You have that game, right, Fred?"

He holds up a plastic case. "Just as you asked, sir. I had to go to several stores before I could find one. These kids are obsessed with video games."

I smile again. Sam and I aren't exactly kids. We're just both a little antisocial. Although most would say he has more reason than I do. There's really no reason for me to seclude myself from the world.

The thought raises all kinds of uncomfortable feelings and memories that I just don't want to deal with. I read work emails on my phone instead, while

Fred weaves in and out of traffic, cursing at the drivers around us. Somehow, he always manages to get us safely to the airport.

When I board the plane, the pilot greets me as usual and updates me on the weather conditions. I sigh as I settle into my seat with a glass of bourbon. No one else is on the plane. I feel an unfamiliar stab of loneliness. Sometimes I feel like my life is a spinning record that always plays the same song.

The flight to Utah is smooth. It helps when you have your own plane and pilot on standby. I step off the plane and relax as I inhale the fresh Southern Utah air. The sky is blue as far as the mountains will let me see.

My silver Jaguar is waiting for me when I arrive. It's next year's model, the F-Type SVR. I design cars that drive themselves, but I love the feel of my hands on the wheel when I'm driving this beast. The private airport is only thirty miles from Moab, and I step on the gas. I turn on the soundtrack from *Phantom of the Opera* and relax for the first time in days.

Despite the music, my mind wonders. At twenty-eight, I have more money than I'll ever be able to spend in ten lifetimes. After my mother died, when I was eight, my dad's life spun out of control. So my Aunt Lauren took over raising me. She made sure the money from my mom's life insurance policy was spent on the best education money could buy. I know I disappointed her when I dropped out of college my senior year to take over my dad's failing business. But family is family, and I felt like it was the least I could do for my mother. She had taken a lot of pride in our family's success.

In the end, everything I did, I did with my mom in the back of my mind. Even if it was too painful to think about how she died. The night my life changed forever.

Nothing was ever the same once she was gone. Dad lost control of the board of directors and left the company in financial ruin. The bastard hid money in offshore accounts and burdened what remained with outstanding attorney bills. But he didn't care. He was a hollow angry shell of a man. Just existing to breathe, and drink.

I'm sure a psychologist could have a field day with my life. I'm the opposite of my father. Everything is ordered and structured. I cannot tolerate any chaos. It's the only way I know. It keeps me focused, but it also keeps me from being close to anyone. I don't really, care, however. I've never been close to anyone anyway since Mom died. Except for Sam and his mom, Claire. I like spending time with them. They make me feel somewhat normal. My time with them is the best part of my week.

* * *

"WHERE'S THE PIZZA?" Sam says as soon as I walk in the door.

"It will be here in five minutes." I walk over and put the new game in the PlayStation. I plop down next to Sam on the couch." This should keep you busy for a while." I grab a remote." Did you finish your last test today?"

"Yep, I aced it." He says. He doesn't look away from the seventy-inch television.

"Good, you can start working for me soon."

"Ha, we'll see about that." There is a knock at the door." Pizza is here." He says.

"Whatever you do, don't get up." I laugh.

"I doubt that'll be a problem," he says and laughs with me. At first, I was afraid to mention Sam's disability. But he's so open and honest about it, I learned to treat it as lightly as he does.

He always kicks my ass at War Games. "One of these days I am going to beat you," I tell him.

"In your dreams. You suck at these games."

I throw the pizza box down on the coffee table and Sam digs in.

"You eat like an animal. How about a paper plate and napkin?" I retrieve them from the cabinet.

"Oh yeah...." He says through a mouth full of food." Mom is going to be a little later than usual tonight. She's on a date." He smiles.

"She knows I like to run a background check on anyone she dates. Did she leave his information for me?"

"Yea, it's over by my computer. She said not to worry because she already used the program you showed her."

I check the print out myself. He's a banker, about ten years older than her. Everything checks out fine on the surface. I jot down a quick note for her.

"Good girl for doing your research, but next time you call me first. I want to know you're safe," I say to myself.

We finish playing around midnight." We have to get up early tomorrow," I say." Do you have everything ready for our climb?"

"I packed all my gear just like you told me. You know mom isn't happy about us going rock climbing, but I think she worries too much."

"She worries every time I take you on an adventure. But she knows you're in good hands with me."

He says goodnight, and maneuvers his wheelchair from behind the table. I watch him roll down the hallway. The sight always makes my heart hurt.

Even if I didn't cause his accident, I can't help but feel responsible.

I head to the spare bedroom. I usually come here on Friday evening, ever since I took over Rylan Designs, and I built this house for Sam and Claire, so I know my way around. Sam has all the best physical therapy equipment money can buy, and he has made a lot of progress. Guilt and shame brought me to them, but they gave me comfort and forgiveness. And some semblance of what it feels like to truly care about other people.

MORNING COMES QUICKLY. The smell of coffee lures me to the kitchen. Claire is cooking breakfast.

"How was your date?" I say with a grin.

She gives me a hug." It was really fun. I'm glad you approved of my background check." She hands me a cup of coffee.

Claire is a little younger than my mother would have been, had mom lived. She has a great smile and her warmth radiates.

"You know... I'm not happy about your rock climbing expedition today." Her smile turns into a scowl.

"Don't worry. I bought all new equipment for him, and I hired two professional climbers to help. He's been bugging me to take him climbing." I put my arm around her shoulder.

"You know you don't owe us anything, right?" She leans into my shoulder.

"We've been over this a million times." I kiss the top of her head.

"You're such a good man, August. I just wish you had a life of your own." She smiles sadly.

"I have everything I need and want. More than enough. Speaking of needing, I ordered Sam one of my self-driving cars. Had it made to meet all his specific needs." I walk to the table and sit down.

"Thank you so much for everything you do for us," she sits with me.

"How's your car holding up?" I ask her.

"August Tanner Rylan, you are not buying me another car. I have a good job now, thanks to you. I can take care of myself." She points her finger at me.

"Okay, okay." I raise my hands in surrender. I like it when she gets all flustered with me because she uses my full name, just like my mother did. It makes me smile. She's one of the only people who can put me in my place.

"Are you coming to watch us today?" I ask her.

"Not everyone can take a day off to play."

"I could call your boss and insist."

"You'll do no such thing, mister." She waves her finger at me again." Just please promise me you two will be safe. Besides, I don't think I could bear to watch my only son, and you, hanging off of a mountainside."

"I promise. We'll be safe."

Zion is one of my favorite places to rock climb. Normally, I climb by myself, but today there's a team to help Sam. He's all suited up; ready to go. I walk around him and check his gear and safety harness. I bend down and double check the braces on his legs.

"Are you sure you want to wear these for the climb today? You're just now getting used to walking in them. Much less climbing a mountain."

"Yes. I'm fine. My physical therapist said it was a good idea. Can we just get going?" He looks up the side of the mountain with a huge smile on his face.

As always, I love his enthusiasm. "Are you not nervous about this at all?"

"I've wanted to do this for years, you know that. I've studied all your climbing videos. Read everything you've given me. Besides, I have you, and those climbing experts to help me. So no, I'm not afraid."

All the hooks, anchors, and ropes are in place. I start my climb first, but I don't move too far ahead in case I need to help him. Sam follows me, flanked by two professional climbers. I see him turn on the Go camera I bought him. He wants to document everything and put it on Youtube.

I make it up the first leg without any issues. I sit on the ledge and watch Sam climb. His progression is slow, but he's doing it. His braces scrape the rock as his climbs, and he fusses at one of the climbers for trying to help him too much. I'm so proud of him. This is what a father must feel like, even if he is only eight years younger than me.

Sam reaches my ledge." I made it."

I laugh." You know we're only halfway up the mountain."

"Thank you so much, August." He hugs me.

"Okay, enough of that. It's going to take us until tomorrow to finish this climb if you don't stop hugging me."

"Well, get your ass off this ledge and quit waiting for me. I may have to pass you."

I start climbing but look back to watch him scanning the majestic scenery with his camera. I'm glad that I could make this happen for him. He is pure joy to me.

* * *

AN HOUR LATER, I reach the top of the mountain. I take a long drink of water, and then pour some on my head. The heat is killer. As I squint into the glare of the mountains, I see two women a few feet away from me. Both are very fit looking. They must've just finished their own climb. One of them removes her helmet. She's stunningly beautiful, with powder blue eyes. She smiles at me as she walks by, and my heart flutters— a wholly unusual feeling for me.

I keep watching her, but she doesn't look at me again. She's too busy watching the mountains. She makes me feel a little unsteady. Or maybe the heat is getting to me.

Sam is yelling at me. He's almost to the top. I grasp his hand to help him with this last mighty effort. He wiggles over the edge and uses his powerful arms to prop himself in a sitting position. He sways as if he's dancing while sitting down. "Whoop Whoop!I made it all the way to the top, man. Help me up. I want to walk around."

I help him stand on his braces and slowly, one

step at a time he makes it to where we can get the best view. Fortunately, it's right beside that pretty blonde. She smiles up at me and congratulates Sam on his climb. She has the sexiest southern drawl. Sam starts flirting with her. I nudge him in the ribs and it doesn't slow him down at all. She chats with him easily, as if she doesn't have a care in the world, and I can do nothing but stare at those powder blue eyes. Woman don't make me speechless, but this particular little blonde has me inarticulate.

She sticks her hand out and introduces herself to Sam." I'm Nashville, and this is my friend Anna."

Instead of shaking her hand, Sam kisses it and bows to her." It's my pleasure to meet you, ladies. This is my tongue-tied friend August."

I want to push his ass off of this mountain, but I manage a "hello." She just smiles and continues paying attention to Sam. Finally, it seems like the small talk is all talked out, and they get ready to head back down the mountain.

"It was very nice to meet both of you,"Nashville says. She turns her back to us and focuses on her equipment.

"We need to get going too if we want to make it back down before dark."

He elbows me." She was hot. You should've gotten her phone number, man."

"Who could ask anything with all that blabbering you were doing? Besides, what's wrong with you, why didn't you get her number for you? You seemed to like her?"

"I was just being nice. She's not my type." He glances down at his legs.

"Sam, you can have any woman you want, don't let anything get in your way." I pat his shoulder.

"I'm not man, I just think she'd be perfect for you. I already have my eye on someone in my statistics class." He nudges me.

"I don't have a type or time for a woman in my life."

"It might help get that stick out of your ass."

I laugh at him." I'd rather spend time with you. Now let's get the hell off this mountain before your mother sends out a search team."

"August." He grabs my arm.

"What?"

"Thank you for today."

"It was my pleasure," I say as I fasten his helmet.

"Are you guys ready for him?" I call down to the climbing guides. They give me the thumbs up. As Sam maneuvers into position his brace gets caught on a rock.

"August, I'm stuck." He tugs at his leg with his hand.

"Hold on a minute. I'll get it." I climb down to him and do my own tugging, but his leg is tightly wedged between two rocks. I tie myself off and tug harder. My hand somehow gets caught up in the metal workings of the brace, ripping a deep gash from just above my thumb downward to my wrist.

"Shit!" I yell as blood rushes down my forearm.

Sam turns around to see what I'm yelling about." I'm so sorry!"

"It's not your fault," I say through gritted teeth. I grab a bandana from my bag and wrap it around my hand. Being left handed is going to make my climb down a little more difficult.

"You're loose now, so try to move again."

"Are you going to be okay?"

"I'll deal with it when our feet are on the ground."

THE CLIMB down for Sam is much easier. The climbers built a pulley system for him. On the other hand, my hand is throbbing, and the bandana is soaked in blood. I leave bloody handprints in my wake. This time, Sam is waiting for me.

"How's your hand?" He takes my hand at the wrist and turns it over.

"I don't know. I haven't looked at it since I wrapped it."

"Can I help?"

I hear that sweet southern drawl, and turn to stare into the big blue eyes of the pretty blonde woman from the precipice.

"I saw the blood path and thought I'd see if I could help you," she says.

Once again, I'm dumbstruck.

She looks at me like she owes me an explanation." I'm sorry...I forget to mention that I'm an ER nurse. I see a lot of trauma. Do you mind if I look at it?"

She asks sweetly through her pink lemonade colored lips.

I extend my hand and nod. She takes gloves from her backpack and gently unwraps my hand. She washes it out with water and I try not to wince.

"You're going to need to have your hand scanned

to make sure you didn't sever any tendons. And you need a lot of stitches."

I hear nothing but the sound of my name on her lips. Everything after that was just noise. What the hell is wrong with me?

"August, did you hear what the pretty lady said?" asks Sam. "We need to take you to the hospital."

That jars me. I hate hospitals. Bad memories from long ago. Just the smell of a hospital is enough to remind me of the worst night of my life. I was only eight, but I can remember every detail. I shake my head to expel those old thoughts and feelings. "Nah," I say. "I'll deal with it myself after we get you home."

Nashville raises her eyebrows. "I don't think you can deal with this yourself. I wouldn't wait too long. You need some antibiotics and if you wait, you won't be able to get that sewn up."

"I'll go as soon as I deliver him back home,"I say too firmly. Her eyes make me forget, just for a moment, why I hate hospitals. No one has ever had that effect on me.

"I actually volunteered to cover for someone for a couple hours tonight. Why don't you meet me at Moab General after you get Sam home?"

"We'll see," I say. I want to see her, but the idea is also terrifying. I feel confused, so I do what I always do when emotions start piling up. I get away from the source of them. "Sam, let's get going. Your mom will be worried."

* * *

I GET Sam loaded into the car and get behind the wheel." Why were you so rude to her, man?" He frowns. "She was just trying to help."

"I hate hospitals, besides, I have my own physician. He can assess what needs to be done." Once I'm away from her big blue eyes, the effect fades, and the old fear of hospitals creeps back.

"I've seen your doctor. He's not near as pretty as that nurse."

"I don't need a pretty little nurse. Just drop it." I glare at him.

"Suit yourself." He leans his head against the window and doesn't utter another word until we make it home. Then he doesn't shut up. He pulls his camera out as soon as we go through the door. He talks a mile a minute as he shows Claire the footage from his big day. Once he runs out of information about our climb, he starts in about my hand.

Claire walks over to look at it. She scowls. "Nasty. Wow. You need to go to the hospital."

"I'll clean it up when I get home. It will be fine." I pull my hand away from her grasp.

"That's not what Nashville said," Sam says with a smirk.

"Who's Nashville?" Claire asks.

"Nobody," I say as I head for the door.

"Thank you for taking Sam today and for keeping him safe."

"You're welcome. I'll be back next week for his graduation." She follows me out.

"August?" She says from behind me.

I feel a lecture coming on." What?"

"If that were Sam's hand, what would you do?" She brushes my cheek.

Shit. Why did she have to play that card?" Okay, you win. After I change clothes I'll get it looked at."

She kisses my cheek and walks toward the house." I'll check on you tomorrow."

Sam wheels into the doorway. The bastard flicks me off and laughs. I should have pushed him off the ledge when I had the chance.

CHAPTER TWO

AUGUST

My house has a gated entry and sits half a mile back onto my property. The view from every window: red mountains. Stella, my housekeeper, always has the place lit up like a landing strip. I'm not sure why, but I think she's scared of intruders. I have a state of the art security system, designed by yours truly. I hit the garage door opener and slide my Jag into its pristine place. I head upstairs to check on the man who has made my life hell since I was eight years old. My father.

His aide stands as I enter the room. "Good evening, Mr. Rylan."

"How was he today?" I ask.

"The same as always. No problems."

If she only knew how much of a problem this

man has been for me, she'd choose different words." I'll check on him tomorrow." Like I always do. Nothing changes. He's always there. Silent and still in the bed, for years. I often think, with a mix of anger, sadness, and bitter irony, that he's much more pleasant in his comatose state than he was when he was conscious.

I head to the shower and exhaustion takes over. That's until I momentarily forget about my hand and rub it through my hair. *Shit, that stings.* Pink tinges the water that runs over my chest. I hold my hand out in front of me. It's filleted all the way down the palm, and the swelling is increasing. I finish showering and towel off. Wiping the steam from the mirror, I lean onto the sink.

I hadn't been in a hospital for years since I was a kid. The last time, I had surgery on my eye. It left my pupil irregular shaped. My eyes are so dark brown that it looks like my pupil bleeds outward and down into the white of my eye. When I was a young, other kids would ask me all the time what happened to my eye? Why does your eye look funny? Every time they'd ask it would shoot pain straight to my heart at the loss of my mother.

One day I finally screamed at this kid who kept teasing me about my eye. His name was Timmy; I'll never forget his bright red hair and buck teeth. "My mother is dead! She died in a car accident, and I almost died too! So my eye is screwed up! Shut up about it!"

Then I ran out of the classroom, crying. I remember running out onto the playground with that whole terrible night flashing before my eyes again. My father and mother screaming at each other in the car. Her telling him to slow down. "Slow down, you're drunk!" She grabbed his arm, but he pushed her away. The car swerved toward the curb.

I called out to her, "Mommy, I'm scared!" And I started crying.

She tried to comfort me, but my father turned around and screamed at me. "Will you shut up? I'm trying to drive!"

And then the crash.

I stared at my reflection in the mirror. My weird eye. The only physical reminder of that night, but what happened lingered in my mind, no matter how I tried to suppress it.

Technically I lost my dad that day, too. He blamed me for the accident. I know he did. And I blamed myself. Why was I such a cry baby? I should've just kept quiet, and he wouldn't have been so distracted. Even if he was drunk, it's not like he never drove drunk before that night. It was his crying son who pushed him over the edge. I took up wearing an eye patch for a while after mom died. I pretended to be a pirate because pirates were tough. That and the fact that I wouldn't talk to anyone didn't exactly gain me a lot of friends and girlfriends. I became comfortable being a loner. It was easier.

I wrap some gauze around my hand and decide to go pay Nashville a visit rather than bothering my doctor this time of night. In all honesty, I wouldn't mind finding out a little more about the baby blue-eyed nurse, and after all this time, I should be able to brave a hospital for an hour.

I'm distracted by delicious smells coming from the kitchen, so I stop for a bite. I ate a few power bars during the climb, but that's it, and I'm starving.

"It's about time you came downstairs. I was beginning to think your sniffer was broken," Stella says and winks.

"It smells wonderful, what is it?" I sit down at the kitchen bar.

Before she turns around she pours me a bourbon. She starts to tell me what she's cooking but stops when she sees my hand.

"What have you done?"

"It's just a cut. As soon as I've consumed massive

amounts of whatever you have cooked, I'm driving myself to the hospital."

"It must be bad if you're going to the hospital." She talks as she fills my plate with eggplant parmesan.

I dig in and ask her about her day between bites of food. Stella is from Italy. Her family came to America when she was a kid. She is funny, when she gets flustered at me she starts speaking Italian. When she first started working for me, I didn't understand a word she was saying, so I started learning Italian on my flight to and from Seattle every week. She was shocked when I responded to her rant one day.

She and her husband live at the back end of my property on the lakeside. He keeps the grounds for me and washes and waxes my car. They're both in their mid-sixties and work harder than most people half their age.

As I'm eating, she washes the dishes and stocks the refrigerator with leftovers." Can I drive you back to your house before I leave?"

"Don't be silly. I have the golf cart. I'll just finish up in here. What would you like for breakfast?"

"I'm more than capable of making my own breakfast, Stella. Take the morning and sleep in." I hand her my plate.

"Thank you, Mr. Ryland, but there is too much to be done to be lazy."

I've tried multiple times to get her to call me August, but she refuses." You're definitely not lazy." I pat her arm. "Good night. Dinner was excellent as usual."

Before I pull out of my drive I contemplate if I should go to the closest hospital, or go out of my way to get another look at those blue eyes. My head tells me just to go to the local hospital, but my other head tells me to go find the girl. Guess who wins out? I feel like I'm driving straight into trouble, and trouble has a name. Nashville.

Thirty minutes later I pull into Moab General. I walk into a packed waiting room. People are hacking and sniffling all over the place. I walk up to the lady manning the check-in desk. She ignores me.

"Excuse me," I say, "I'm here to see Nashville."

"Nash is busy. You'll have to wait your turn."

"She told me to come and see her. I cut my hand." I hold my hand up for her to see.

She doesn't even look up from her computer."

Look, mister, unless you're having chest pains, you'll have to wait your turn."

The double doors open and Nashville walks into the waiting room with a patient, an older man. I stand and watch her.

"Excuse me, sir," says the clerk, "but you need to fill out this paperwork."

Now she decides to pay attention to me. I take them from her and hear, "August?"

I turn around. Nashville stands a few feet away from me. I hold up my hand." I decided to take your advice, but it looks like I may need to come back tomorrow."

She leans close to me. So close I can smell her. She smells of mango." Follow me." She whispers. She grabs the clipboard of paperwork and places it back on the desk.

"He has to fill out the paperwork, Nash, and he can't just go in front of all these people who have been waiting." The pleasant desk lady looks like she's about to grab my arm and toss me back into the waiting room.

Nashville grabs the clipboard back off the desk, flashes a smile at her grim colleague, and drags me through the double doors.

* * *

"I'm glad you decided to come in," she says. "I was worried that you wouldn't. Can you fill out the paperwork while I get someone to help us?" She drags me into another room. It looks cold and sterile.

"I'm left-handed." I hold up my injured hand.

"Oh, sorry. Here, let me have it." She starts writing." August. . . What's your last name?" She stops and looks at me with those big powder blue eyes.

"Rylan."

She writes again." Address and phone number?"

I give them to her.

"Insurance?"

"Cash."

"Are you sure? The scan will be expensive. I can see if you will qualify for any help?"

"Do I look like I need help?" I ask.

"I'm sorry. I guess not," she says in that southern drawl.

I think I've hurt her feelings. I just restate "cash."

She looks down only at the paper now." Any medical history?"

This is none of her fucking business. I'm getting defensive. "No."

"What happened to your eye?" Now her blues have found mine.

I look down and pick something imaginary off my pants." Birth defect." It's a lie, but a plausible one.

"Okay, Mr. Rylan, I think I have enough to get started. Let me go get some orders, and I'll have someone take you to the CT Scan."

I guess I've pissed her off. Now I am Mr. Rylan, but suddenly I'm in a panic." No."

She stops in her tracks." No what?"

"If you can't take me, I'm out of here." I get up to leave.

She squints at me, and then stands close to me with her hands on her hips." Do you just like being in control, or are you scared?"

"I'm not afraid of anything." That's the second time I have lied to her.

"Well, if you were scared, I'd just go with you, but since it is a control issue, you're on your own." She walks out.

Shit. That backfired. This blue eyed southern spitfire has single handedly taken my control away. I start to hyperventilate. I'm a grown damn man. I can handle this. Both my hands are pulling at my hair when she walks back in with a transporter and a wheelchair. She looks at me wide-eyed.

"Um.... It's okay," she says to the transporter. "I'll take him. I'm sure you have other patients you can transport."

Relief washes over me and I relax.

"Sit down, August." Her voice is much softer, and she points to the wheelchair.

I don't say anything, but I sit. We enter the elevator and she pushes the floor number. "So, it wasn't a control issue. You were actually scared." She whispers it." Or maybe it's a little of both." She states the last part a little louder.

"What kind of name is Nashville?" I ask, just to try to change the subject.

"What kind of name is August?"

Damn, this woman cuts me no slack. I've never met a woman like her." My mother thought August was the most beautiful time of year." For some reason, I answered her truthfully. I don't think I've ever shared that with anyone since she died.

The doors open, thank god. She knocks on the door to let the tech know we're here and ready for the scan." Come lay down on this. Your body will go through this tube until your hand is under it."

I lay on the hard, narrow bed. She hasn't taken

her eyes off of me. Then I hear her softly say, "I'm from Nashville, Tennessee. It is my father's favorite place in the world. He said he loved it so much that he wanted to name his most prized possession after his favorite place." She smiles shyly at me.

Damn. She is beautiful.

We return to the cold sterile room. She has been quiet since she told me about her name." Wait here while I go get some supplies and a physician." She comes back with a doctor who introduces himself, but my attention is solely on her.

"Did you hear him, August?" She touches my arm and it feels she burned me. I've had sex with many women. None of them scorched my skin like she just did.

"Sorry, no." I look directly at her.

"He said the tendons and ligaments are all intact, but you will need several stitches, antibiotics, and a tetanus shot." She touches my arm again and this time, it feels like electrical energy flowing up my arm.

"Okay."

"If it's okay with you, I'll stay here with you until

the doctor is done." Now she's holding my hand. Is she trying to comfort me, or appease me? Either way, I don't want her to leave.

As promised, she held my hand during the entire procedure. I clasped hers back, and I never took my eyes off of her. For some reason, I find her fascinating. The southern drawl thing is such a turn on. I need to find out more about this woman. The only thing I know we have in common is mountain climbing, but maybe there's more.

The doctor finishes and leaves, and Nashville dresses my hand. She bites the inside of her bottom lip as she concentrates. I smile up at her.

"What?" she asks me.

"You're good at what you do aren't you?"

"I hope so. I enjoy taking care of people."

That gives me an idea, but I need to check her background first.

"All done. Now all you need is your tetanus shot." She unlocks a cabinet and pulls out a labeled syringe. She blushes when she turns back around.

"Um.... I need access to your hip."

She's actually embarrassed. That's a good sign. I stand up and lower my jeans slightly. She's so gentle when she inserts the needle, but it's followed by a burn. I ignore it. It's inconsequential compared to the heat radiating between us.

She takes a small white bottle from the cabinet." Do you have any drug allergies?"

"No."

"You'll need to take these as directed for one week, and then come back here in ten days to remove your stitches." She hands them to me.

"Will you be here?"

"Anyone can help you if I'm not here."

I guess this is where a normal person would ask her for her phone number, but I can't do that until I know more about her." Thank you for your help, Nashville." Her name just rolls off my tongue. I like the way it feels. I'd like to know how she feels underneath those scrubs.

"My pleasure. No mountain climbing until that is completely healed. Tell Sam I said hello." She smiles sweetly.

As soon as I get into my Jag, I call the head of my security detail. I should feel bad about calling him after midnight, but I pay him a lot of fucking money. He can just deal with it.

He sounds tired when he answers the phone." Mr. Rylan."

"Good evening, Wayne. I need you to do a complete background check on Nashville...." It dawns on me that I don't know her last name. There can't be that many people with that name.

"Do you have the last name for me, sir?"

"No, but I know she is from Nashville Tennessee and she's a nurse working out of Moab General. That should be enough for you to go on. I want the information on my computer by tomorrow morning."

"Will do, sir."

CHAPTER THREE

NASH

The apartment light is still on. I walk in, and Anna is laying on our beat up old denim couch watching a movie.

"You're up late." I put down my purse and join her on the end of the couch.

"I was waiting up for you. Like you do for me when I work a crazy shift." She sits up.

She works odd shifts to make extra money to buy all the clothes and shoes that she craves. I work extra shifts to help my parents try to save their farm back in Tennessee. Daddy isn't able to do it all alone anymore, so he had to hire some help and the weather the last couple years has wrecked havoc on the farming business. Momma says they're barely staying afloat, and they're in jeopardy of losing the farm that has been in our family for a hundred years.

I had a blissful childhood. There's just such a freedom about growing up on a farmland, growing your own food, riding horses, herding cattle and collecting eggs from the chickens. Most all of that is gone now. There are only a few cows and chickens left.

"How was your shift?" Anna asks.

"It was a little weird." I scrunch my nose at her and get more comfortable on the couch, drawing my legs underneath me.

"Why, what happened?"

"Remember the two guys we met on our climb today?"

"Yea, the cute young guy with the braces and his totally rocking hot friend." She beams at me.

"Since the totally rocking hot friend injured his hand on the climb down, I told him to come see me in the ER. He showed up at the front desk asking for me."

"So what was so weird? You told him to come and see you."

"Most of the time he just kept staring at me. For some reason, I got the feeling he was terrified to be there, but he came anyway."

She laughs." Have you looked in the mirror lately? I'm sure he was there to see you."

"I thought so at first, but he never asked me for my phone number. He comes across as a city boy and rich, so not my type."

"Last time I checked, you haven't had a type since your first year of college and that didn't work out so well." She pats my hand.

"Yes, but this guy is dark and mysterious. I feel like he's hiding something."

"Dark and mysterious.... tall, dark and handsome, rich... these don't sound like bad things to me Nash. Oh.... I have an idea...let's google him." She hops off the couch and walks over to the computer desk.

"Did you get his last name?"

"This is crazy. I'm sure you're not going to find anything." I join her anyway.

She types August. . . "What's his last name?"

"Rylan." I wait as she enters his name into google.

"Oh my god Nash. He's mega rich. He's the owner of Rylan Designs in Seattle. Look at the size of his building."

I grab a chair from our two seater kitchen table. I read the specs and his building is fifteen stories tall and houses several corporations. His office is on the top floor.

"Enough about the building. Let's check out his profile." She sounds excited. "He's twenty-eight years old, single, took over his father's dying business at twenty-one. Turned it into a thriving empire."

"So, he doesn't even live here?" Now I'm curious.

"That's what you took away from that?"

"Single."

"Single." She states again and points to his profile picture." He's gorgeous. That black hair and aviator sunglasses."

I notice that he's wearing dark glasses in every picture I see of him. More importantly, I see a beautiful woman on his arm in every picture. A different woman in each picture.

"His right eye has a birth defect. That must be why he wears glasses in all his pictures," I say.

"Who gives a shit? He's still totally hot." She keeps flipping through pictures of him.

"Is there anything personal about him?"

She scrolls through a couple of pages." That is strange, it's like he was nonexistent until the age of twenty-one. Except for this." She points to a picture that someone snapped of August standing in front of a headstone holding white canailles. The name on it's Sara Rylan.

I'm curious. "Who do you think that is, a wife, a girlfriend...maybe that's why he's single?"

Anna quickly opens another page and types in Sara Rylan.

"It was his mother." She whispers.

I feel sad for him. I can't imagine my life without my mother in it." Does it mention his father?"

Her fingers quickly continue her search." Huh.... it appears he's dead too. The only thing I found on him is that August took over his business, but it doesn't mention him anywhere else."

"I get the feeling that he's a loner."

"Well for someone that is a loner, I'm sure he has lots of people wanting to be his friend. With his financial status and the fact that he's an eligible bachelor. I'd sure be cozying up to him. His money could fix all my problems." She laughs.

"Anna! That's terrible." I pinch her arm.

"Owe! I love you, but that's the difference between you and me. I'd marry for money. You keep hanging on to marry for love."

"I could never marry someone for his money. I need his heart and soul."

"This's why you will be single for a really long

time. You may even die an old maid." She laughs again.

I hope she's wrong. I want a happy marriage, like my parents. They still hold hands when they walk together. Mom has always said that dad makes her laugh and they have fun together." *Honesty always first,*" she says. He still gives her butterflies when he smiles at her. That's what I want. I don't care if I'm poor. I've never had money, and I've always been happy. Even though money right now would make life easier for my mom and dad. I'm happy just to have a new pair of cowboy boots once a year.

"Maybe I should go after him," Anna says.

"You will do no such thing." I glare at her.

"I think someone likes him."

"No, I just don't want to see you get your claws into him for his money. He's sweet in a strange sort of way. Besides, I probably will never see him again, and we are polar opposites. Like you said, I'm sure he has woman like you falling all over him. What in the world would he want with a country girl like me? I'd never make it in the city."

"Well, you have to admit he is dreamy." She kisses the computer screen.

"You're awful." I laugh at her. I know at heart she is just teasing me. We met our first day of college, and we've been best friends ever since. She comes from a family with money, but they have her on a tight budget to learn the value of it. She's just enrolled to get her masters in nursing. I, on the other hand, am struggling to keep things afloat between my school loans, rent, and helping my parents. There's no room for me to afford to pursue my masters right now. Thankfully, I have an older Mustang that I don't have any payments on, other than an occasional repair. I think only hard work and dedication are in my future.

I lean closer to the computer screen." He *is* very dreamy."

CHAPTER FOUR

AUGUST

Like it does most nights, sleep evades me. I check on my dad and head downstairs. The smell of coffee is a powerful draw for me. Stella has evidently already been here. She has fresh fruit laid out beside a pot of coffee and a mug.

I take it into my office. I'm anxious to get the report from Wayne. My hand is throbbing as I grab the mouse.

Good man, I knew he'd have it for me. I click on the file and there's a picture of her beautiful face.

Nashville Jacoby.

Nurse.

Age 26

George and Nancy Jacoby. Parents. Married 40 years.

No Siblings.

Grew up on a farm outside Nashville, Tennessee.

Bank Account number.

Balance $1,045. 00

Savings $200. 00

Address

Cell phone number

Social Security Number

Drivers License number

RN license number

For a nurse, she should have more money. I keep scrolling down.

Student loans $35,000

Breakdown of how she spends her money.

Transfer of funds every month to parents account $2000. 00

Rent $800. 00

No car payment and no credit cards.

Drives a 2008 Ford Mustang.

. . .

I PULL up the financial reports on her parents. They're behind on all their payments. Their house is not far from foreclosure. It's obviously the reason she sends them money every month.

I keep reading, but nothing else pops out. No arrest records, college GPA, a picture of what appears to be a boyfriend in college. Hopefully, one that's out of the picture. She rides horses, or at least she used to ride. She and Anna appear to be pretty close. There are tons of pictures of them together. The only hobby I see is mountain climbing.

NOTHING UNUSUAL AT ALL. I think I have the perfect job to offer her. My phone rings. "Hello, Wayne."

"Did you get my email, sir?"

"Yea, I did. Thanks for getting it to me so quickly."

"I figured if you called me after midnight it must've been important."

"If you dig up anything else let me know." I hang up and stuff the phone in my pocket. I hear the back door open and the sound of Stella opening cabinets. She looks up when I enter the kitchen.

"Good morning. Wait, why aren't you out for

your run? You run every morning." She puts away groceries as she talks.

"I'm going," I say. "I had something pressing I needed to do this morning."

She shoos her hand at me for trying to help her put away the groceries." This is what you pay me to do, Mr. Rylan. Now go away."

"Are you ever going to call me August?" I give her a charming smile.

"I'll call you August when I know longer work for you, so unless you plan on firing me, you are Mr. Rylan."

"You're fired then."

She turns around and gapes at me.

I put my hand on her shoulder." I'd never fire you. My house would fall down without you. And I don't know how to cook."

"Oh, Mr. Rylan, if I didn't work for you I'd take you over my knee and spank you for giving me a heart attack." Her Italian accent comes out when she's flustered. It's heavy right now. I laugh out loud and kiss her on the cheek.

I STRETCHED, put on my wireless earphones, cranked up *One Republic*, and start my run along the mountain trails. Southern Utah is beautiful. My mind drifts to how I ended up here. It's the one reason I can thank my dad for fucking up so badly. There were so many lawsuits after the car accident, the one that killed my mother and left Sam paralyzed. Dad faced vehicular manslaughter charges because of my mother's death. His name was all over the news. That started the downfall of his company, and our lives. Somehow he avoided any jail time. I'm sure his high paid attorney's got him off. Claire sued him for medical bills for Sam, but somehow the bastard claimed restructuring of his company and filed chapter thirteen. He hid all his money from the courts and didn't have to pay Claire a dime.

I didn't find any of this out until I was in college. On one of my breaks I went to see the old man, and I heard him bragging to one of his friends about it. I was fucking furious with him. When I confronted him about it, he insisted I'd heard him incorrectly, so I did my own digging. The company was broke, but he had taken all the money out of it and put it in offshore accounts. I was an amateur hacker, so I could link the accounts back to him.

When I confronted him again, he kicked me out

of the house. He went on another drinking spree that night and got in another car accident. Even though he was drunk, the other driver was actually at fault. The driver was killed instantly and the family came after Dad in full force. His lawyers protected him again, but his name was once again front page news. My mother's name also smeared all over the paper again.

"Millionaire Tom Rylan owner of Premier Designs in Seattle Washington killed his wife Sara and walked away a free man. Now he's killed again."

I couldn't handle going through my mother's death again. So I devised a plan and quit college. I met him at his house late one night and told him I now had access to his offshore accounts, and I was giving the money to Claire and Sam. That very night, my father had a massive stroke. He hasn't spoken since. I made his mess go away and moved out from under the watchful eye of the city of Seattle. I changed the name of the company and restructured it. Logistically, I needed it to stay in Seattle, but I didn't need to live there to make it work.

I stop for a water break and enjoy my surroundings. As far as the eye can see the red rock of the canyon stands out against the backdrop of the endless blue sky. There's a freedom being outside here, in this place, that I never feel anywhere else.

I sit down on a rock and pull out my cell phone. I programmed her number the minute I saw it on the computer.

* * *

"Hello," she says.

"Nashville, this is August."

"How did you get this number?"

"I'm a man of many means." I don't give her time to respond." I have a job offer for you."

"I already have a job I love."

"I think you will at least want to consider it. The pay is outstanding."

"This is just a little weird, don't you think?"

"Meet me for dinner and we can discuss it."

"I don't think so...."

I interrupt her." Let me start over. Will you please let me take you to dinner tonight to discuss a serious job opportunity?" I'm not accustomed to people turning me down.

"You mean like a date?"

She's so frustrating." No, not a date. I don't date my employees."

"You want me to work for you? I'm a nurse, not a car designer."

I never told her what I do for a living. She must have googled my name. Good thing people only see what I want them to see.

I try for very sweet." I promise you. It's in your field of expertise."

She pauses and I hold my breath." Okay," she finally says. "Where do you want to meet?"

"I'll pick you up at seven. Wear something casual."

"Let me guess. You don't need my address because you already have it?"

I could lie to her and tell her I don't." I have it."

"Well put this on your list of discussions tonight. Stalking is not allowed!" She sounds curt. It's kind of a turn on.

"Duly noted." I hang up before she has a chance to change her mind.

STELLA IS VACUUMING when I return from my run. I pull the plug out of the wall, and she starts shaking the vacuum cleaner, trying to make it turn back on. I laugh and she turns around.

"You're nothing but trouble today, Mr. Rylan." She says with her hands on her hips.

"I hate to cause more trouble for you today, but do you think you could make dinner for two, around eight o'clock?"

She sashays over to me." Now this is interesting." She's teasing me.

"You never have guests. Except for Mr. Sam, of course. Will he be joining you? I like him. He picks on you."

"That he does, but no. Sam will not be joining us. This is a business dinner."

"Does this dinner guest happen to be of the female persuasion?" Her voice just went up a few octaves.

I call back to her, "It's a business meeting Stella. Nothing more."

THE SHOWER REMOVES the sweat and grime from my run. I wrap a towel around my waist and open my massive walk-in closet. I have rows of expensive suits. Suits for work, suits for entertaining clients, and tuxedos for the elaborate affairs that I'm obligated to attend. I told Nashville casual, so I opt for a pair of jeans and a black button-down shirt. No tie.

I study my face in the mirror. I have a pretty thick five o'clock shadow from not being able to shave with my injured hand. I'm always so clean shaven. The all-American boy. This is definitely a different look on me. Why am I so nervous? It's not like I haven't conducted employee interviews in my home office before. I do a background check on all employees that work in my home. But this is an unusual scenario anyway. She wasn't applying for a job until I offered it to her, and I've never had any job candidates for dinner, much less have job interviews inspire me to contemplate whether or not to shave my face. I briefly wonder what my scruffy face would feel like against the soft skin of her cheek or better yet, the inside of her thigh. I really need to get my shit together when it comes to this woman. I'm a grown damn man, but I've never been in love. I've had plenty of sex, but it has always been emotionlessness. Just an act. I've enjoyed it but never had a real connection. These feelings make me anxious.

I dial up Sam and put him on speaker phone while I get dressed.

"Hey, how is your hand?" he asks. "Did you go see that pretty southern nurse?"

Straight to the point." Yes, I did, and my hand hurts. How did your physical therapy go today?"

"I was able to walk the length of my driveway with my braces on." I can hear the smile in his voice.

"That's great. Before you know it you won't even need your wheelchair anymore."

"Did you ask her out?"

"Actually, I'm picking her up at seven, and I'm bringing her to my house for dinner."

"Wow, you must really like her. You never invite girls over."

"It's not what you think. I'm going to ask her to work for me."

He is quiet for a moment." That must mean you want her to take care of your dad. I don't think that is such a good idea. She might expose you, and ruin everything you have worked for. You know I don't like your father, but I don't want to see anything happen to you. Can't you just date her?"

I appreciate the fact that Sam wants to protect me." I have it covered. Don't worry. I need to go or I'll be late picking her up. I'll see you next Friday."

. . .

THE THIRTY-MINUTE DRIVE goes by too quickly. I pull up at her apartment complex and see her old Mustang. There's a cowboy hat perched up in the back window, and a sticker on her bumper that says *"save a horse ride a cowboy."*

Fuck. I'm not a cowboy. The apartments look well maintained, but I don't see any security measures in place. I walk up the three flights of stairs and find her apartment at the end of the hall. I raise my hand to knock and the door flies open.

Anna, who only stands about an inch shorter than my six one frame, greets me with a mischievous grin.

"Hi August, remember me?"

"Yes, I do." I reach to shake her hand and she grabs me into a hug. Someone needs to teach this woman about personal space. As I awkwardly pull out of her embrace, I see Nashville standing behind her laughing.

She looks beautiful. She has on a simple pale blue dress that matches her eyes. As I scan her body downward, she has on cowboy boots. I don't think I've ever even seen anyone in that kind of boots. Fuck me boots, yea, but not those. Somehow she makes them look sexy. Her dress is cut showing just the right amount of cleavage. She has a small waist and curvy hips. She's much shorter than Anna. Her long blonde hair is down with some curls at the end. I like that she barely has any makeup on, except for those lips. She has a soft pink shade on that makes her lips look so damn fuckable.

"You look nice." I smile at her.

"Thanks, so do you." I see her scan my body as well.

"You two kiddos have fun." Anna flips past me apparently heading out for a run.

"So are you ready?" I'm suddenly anxious about being alone with her.

"Let me grab my purse and lock up."

I put out my elbow to walk her down the stairs and I get that same electrical feeling I did when she touched me in the hospital. I wonder if she feels it too, or if it's just me.

I open the Jag door and she doesn't move.

"Have you changed your mind?" I frown at her. Please don't change your mind.

"No, I'm just surprised this is your car. I thought we'd be riding in one of your designs. Is this what you drive every day?"

I'm confused. I look at the Jag and then back at her." You don't like it?"

"No.... it's beautiful. I'm.... . just a little afraid to sit in it. Maybe I should go change my clothes."

I laugh out loud at her. "You look perfect. Just get in the car."

She finally climbs in and I reach in and buckle her seatbelt. I climb on my side and do the same. She fidgets with her dress and bites her lip. Music always relaxes me, so I turn on XM radio to one of my all-time favorites: Frank Sinatra.

She laughs." You like Sinatra?"

I smile back at her." Who doesn't?"

"You'd get along with my father. I grew up listening to his music."

A farmer and I have something in common. Who would've thought? Maybe we're not so different after all. I put the car in gear and ease out onto the main road.

"So where are you taking me for this business meeting?" She looks at me.

"To my house." I'm glad I have my aviator glasses on so she can't see how nervous I am about bringing her to my home.

"Wait. What? I thought this was a business meeting."

"It is. I conduct business at my house all the time."

"Don't you live in Seattle?"

I glance over at her." What makes you think I live in Seattle?"

"That's where your company is located."

"Who has been stalking whom now?" I ask.

"Anna!" She blurts out." She made me check you out." Her hands are clasped together and her knuckles are turning white.

I reach over and place my hand on hers." It's okay. I was only teasing you. You should check anyone out before you get involved with him." I realize as I said that last part that it was a poor choice of words.

"Is that what we are doing? Getting involved?"

"No.... I meant anyone that you are going to work for." Why do I let her get me so flustered?" Just so you know, I do have an office here in Moab. I work out of there Tuesday through Friday. I'm only in Seattle on Mondays.

She looks straight ahead and is quiet for the next long thirty minutes. I watch her periodically from behind my glasses. She has a slight frown on her face like she's thinking hard about something. Just as we're about to turn into my driveway, she blurts out,

"Can you at least tell me what the job is?" Then her eyes get big as she sees the gated entrance." You live here?"

"It's just a house. I'll explain everything while we eat."

I don't pull into the garage, instead, I park out front. I get out and open her car door.

"This place is beautiful," she says.

Almost as beautiful as you, I think, but I keep my mouth shut.

CHAPTER FIVE

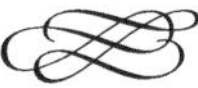

NASH

His house is a mansion. His car alone says it all. Money. He opens the car door for me and reaches across me to unbuckle my seatbelt. He smells so good, and I have butterflies from his touch. Everything about him is so overwhelming, but I find myself drawn to him. or maybe it's just curiosity. He's far away out of my playing field. I'm used to pickup trucks and barns.

His front yard has a fountain. A huge damn fountain that spurts colored water into the air. It's beautiful, but I don't really see the purpose. He grabs my hand and it feels possessive and confident. I need to remember this is a business meeting. He walks me into the house, and it's equally overwhelming. It's very modern, with an immense artisan chandelier in the entryway. To the left, I see what looks like an office with an extensive library.

He continues to hold my hand and walks me straight to the back of the house, into a large kitchen with an island bar for seating and a great room off to the side. The entire back of the house is lined with large glass doors that open up to a deck area with an infinity pool, complete with a cabana. Something I've seen only in magazines.

My eye catches the only piece of furniture that doesn't fit in. It is an old piano that sits in one of the corners of the room. It doesn't look like it has been used in years. There are a few pictures scattered on top of it. The room is decorated in blues and browns. The couch consumes half of the room. It's all-white and L-shaped with large cushions. On the wall hangs a gigantic television set. I suddenly feel completely out of place here. I start to fidget.

I hear a clinking noise behind me. There's a woman in the kitchen stirring a pot. August releases my hand and heads to the bar." Is dinner ready, Stella?"

"Five more minutes, Mr. Rylan." She clears her throat." Why don't you ask your guest if she'd like a drink?"

"I'm sorry Nashville, this is Stella. She's my

housekeeper, cook, and a lifesaver." He smiles shyly.

"It's very nice to meet you, Ms. Nashville,"Stella says politely.

"Its nice to meet you too, please just call me Nash." She extends her hand to me.

"Good luck with that." He laughs." She has worked for me for years and I can't get her to use my first name.

"Nash, would you like some wine?" Stella asks me and winks. August's mouth is hanging open, and I laugh despite my nerves.

"I'd love a glass of anything you have that's white." I lean into August. "I like her."

"She has just moved down on the list of my favorite people." He says teasingly.

Stella pulls her lasagna-laden spoon out of the pan and points it at him.

"You be careful Mr. Rylan; I could put some really bad things in your food."

I laugh out loud again, which seems to be infectious because they both start laughing.

All is forgiven when Stella hands him a bourbon and glass of white wine. He pulls out the chair at the bar for me to sit down and he sits beside me. Stella dishes up a colorful salad.

"Thank you," I say. She smiles sweetly at me. I

wait to eat as I watch her fill our plates with lasagna. It smells heavenly, and she adds what looks to be homemade bread with butter. I wipe my mouth just in case I'm drooling.

"Thank you for all of your hard work Stella," August says. I think he's hinting that it's time for her to leave.

She places the pans back in the oven." If you need anything else, you know where to find me." She opens the back door." Or you can do it yourself as you often tell me." She winks at him this time and disappears.

"I really do like her." I smile at him and start eating my salad.

"She's awesome. She doesn't put up with my shit."

"She seems to really like you, and you're very comfortable with her."

"Yea, I guess I am."

I steal a bite of my lasagna." Oh my god, this is the best thing I've ever put in my mouth." I see his eyes dilate and wonder what he's thinking.

"I love your house," I say, going back to safer territory. "How many stories is it?"

"Three." He says between bites.

"How many people live here?"

"Do you mean live in the house, or live on the property?"

"Inside the house."

"Two." He starts eating again.

Maybe Stella lives in here. He didn't volunteer information, and I don't want to pry." I love the old piano."

His fork stops midair." It was my mother's."

"I'm sorry. I saw a picture on the internet where you were visiting her grave."

He stops eating and walks over to the glass doors. He glares out at the mountains.

I wipe my hands and face and walk up beside him." Did I say something wrong?" His whole demeanor has changed. His beautiful smile is gone.

He breathes out really hard." No, I can't blame you for researching me when I did the same to you."

"I think your stalkery was a little more in depth than me googling a few things."

He visibly relaxes and turns toward me." Mine was extensive because I want you to work for me."

"Can we finish our meal before we finish this conversation?" I take his hand and walk him back over to the bar.

* * *

We finish our food and end up on the couch." So what is this position you have for me?" I can't imagine what he's going to say.

"I need a full-time nurse on staff."

"In Seattle? At your design company?"

"No, here at my house."

"I don't get it."

"For my father. He had a major stroke a while ago and I've been taking care of him ever since. I need someone here five days a week while I work. The nurse that had been taking care of him retired."

"August, I have a full-time job that I love. Besides, I was under the impression that your father was dead." This really is a business meeting. I had hopes that maybe it was a little more. Stupid me for thinking that he really liked little ole country me.

"For all intents and purposes, he is. As far as the world knows, he is dead. I'll make it worth your while. Every year my company gives out scholarships solely for nurses. I was in an unfortunate accident when I was young and had to spend some time in the hospital. The nurses took such good care of me. It's my way of paying it forward. You can use the scholarship to pay off your student loans. I'll pay you double what the hospital pays you."

Holy shit, he's serious." Why me?"

"Because I was very impressed by how you took care of me. I need that care for my father."

I get up and start pacing." I don't know August, I.... ."

"You could use the money to help your parents before their house goes up for foreclosure."

I walk back over to him." Give it to me!"

His turn to look confused." Give you what?"

"The fucking file you have on me."

He looks angered for a moment but gets up and walks out of the kitchen toward his office. I don't follow him.

He comes back with a folder and hands it to me. He still looks pretty pissed off." You need to watch your mouth." He states flatly.

"You are unreal." I open the file and look at all the information he has on me." You can have every detail of my life in a folder and I can't say the word fuck! Well fuckity, fuck fuck!" I know it was childish, but I'm infuriated.

He takes a deep breath and starts counting. He makes it to ten and seems much calmer. "Let's both sit down and try this again."

I sit down and throw the folder on the coffee table. I cross my arms across my chest.

"I have to fully investigate all my employees."

"I didn't apply for a job with you. You sought me out and had already gathered all of this information on me. There's a difference."

"Okay. I get why you're angry."

I think he's lying. I don't think he gets any of it. I think he's so used to being in control and getting whatever he wants that he has no clue how to interact with other people. It's kind of sad really. I soften just a little toward him.

"August." I touch his hand." If you want to know something about me just ask me. I'm pretty much an open book. I've nothing to hide."

"I'll try to remember that in the future." His shoulders relax. "So will you take the job?"

I really would like to help my parents and pay off all my school loans. It'd be nice to be debt free, and save my parents' farm.

"Yes. I accept the position."

"Good. Before we go any further I need you to sign a nondisclosure." He hands me a paper out of the folder.

"I don't understand. What's there for me to tell?"

"Unlike you, I do have secrets about my family. I can't risk them coming out. You can't tell anyone my father is alive." He watches me carefully as he hands me a pen.

I sign it." I'd never tell your secrets anyway."

"Not even to Anna?" He stares at me waiting for my response.

"Not even Anna. What goes on in your household is yours to own. It's nobody else's business, but I'll have to be inventive when it comes to what exactly I'm doing for you as a nurse. I stand." Can you take me home? I think I've had enough fun for one night."

"We need to go over some details."

"You can fill me in on the drive home."

I LISTEN to him talk for thirty minutes. He has a lot of demands. I need to give two weeks' notice right away. He wants me to live at his house in the spare room across from his father. I only agreed to live there during the week while I was working. He doesn't own my weekends.

This whole night was not what I envisioned at all. Yes, I ended up getting a really good job, but at what cost? I was stupid to think there was anything between us. I'm admittedly a little disappointed, but at least I know where I stand with him now.

CHAPTER SIX

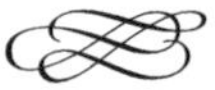

AUGUST

The week has flown by. Sam's high school graduation is tonight. He's a smart kid, but he fell behind when he had surgery at sixteen to try to improve his lower body movements. He ended up with an infection, which delayed his recovery, but in the end, it did improve his mobility. He mentally gave up for about a year. Claire and I pushed him like crazy. He finally turned around, and he's made so much progress.

I tease him about working for me, but I really want him to go to college. He's a wiz at the computer, and with a minimal amount of guidance, he'll do great things. I have given him some mock projects from work. I've been highly impressed with his skills.

I've been busy at work all week working on a

design for a new car manufacturer in Italy. My team flies out today to make sure everything goes smoothly. I called Nashville before my plane took off in Seattle to see how her plans have progressed. I wanted her to come back over to meet my father and the staff that will be working under her. Plus, I really just wanted to see her. She has agreed to meet me at one today. Sam's graduation isn't until six.

My hand is looking much better and not as swollen. I look at myself in the mirror and decide I like my new beard. I'm not ready to shave it. Stella complimented me on it this week.

I flew Fred home with me to help with the driving, so I sent him to pick up Nashville. That was a struggle all in itself. She's not very good at taking orders.

The front door opens and Nashville is calling my name. Stella greets her. I meet up with them in the kitchen. They are already laughing about something.

She looks beautiful as usual, a bit overdressed in black slacks, a blue button-down, and heels. Her hair is pulled back into a ponytail and those damn lips of hers are a soft pink. They are very distracting. I want to taste them.

"Good morning, ladies."

"You missed breakfast this morning, Mr. Rylan.

Can I make you anything?" Stella says as she stands up.

"I'll just have a cup of coffee. Thank you."

"Good afternoon, Mr. Rylan,"Nashville says, and smiles.

"Not you, too."

"All your other employees call you Mr. Rylan, so I figured it was appropriate."

"You figured wrong. You may not call me Mr. Rylan." I'm dead serious.

She puts down her cup of coffee a little too hard and it sloshes over the rim." Okay, August."

"You haven't been here five minutes and you are already angry with me. Why's that?" I stare at her blue eyes.

"I'm not used to being bossed around all the time. Like insisting that I can't drive my own car or that I can't call you Mr. Rylan."

"If you drove your own car you might be late. I'm on a schedule today."

She sits back in her chair. Stella wipes up her spill.

"So are you always so controlling with your employees?" Nashville asks.

"Frankly, yes." I glance at Stella. She's giving me the evil eye. I choose to ignore her.

"Okay then, Mr. Rylan, I came here to meet your father and to see where I'll be living during the week, so can we get on with it. I wouldn't want to mess up your time schedule."

Why do I find her defiance so damn sexy? I smile at her, rather than being angry. She will be a challenge for me. I stand up and pull out her chair and surprisingly she lets me.

"Follow me."

She doesn't answer but she does as I ask. We make it to the third floor and I decide to show her to her room first.

"This will be your room. If there's anything you need, please let Stella know." She walks in and drags her hand on the silk bedspread.

"This is nice. A little too nice for me. Would you mind if I bring my own bedding?"

She doesn't like silk, mental note." Whatever is going to make you comfortable, but if you just give Stella a list, she'll get you whatever you want." I cock my head at her.

She looks at the paintings on the wall." I can't afford to buy all new things right now, so I'll just bring my extra set over."

"I didn't mention you paying for anything Nashville. It is all part of your compensation package." I walk over to her.

"I prefer to pay my own way if that is okay with you. You're already paying me very well."

I don't know what possess me to lose control, maybe it's her fucking pink lemonade lips taunting me, but I grab her and kiss her. She opens to me slightly and I take complete advantage of enjoying her sweet mouth. The intensity between us scares the hell out of me. I've lost control to this southern beauty.

I pull away from her, breathless, and stare down into her eyes. Her lips are even pinker and fuller from me tasting her. What she does to me has me so confused. We both hold our stare for a moment.

"Um...maybe...um. . . you should introduce me to your father." She blushes.

I bite my tongue because all I want to do is consume her again.

"You're right. You can meet your staff too. I had them all join us for your introduction to your new position." I grab her hand but she doesn't budge.

"I have staff?"

"Yes. He has round the clock nursing assistants caring for him. I need you to manage his care, and their care of him."

She looks puzzled." So what do you need me for if it's all already being taken care of?"

"I need you to take care of his medical issues and manage his medications. Make sure the staff is meeting all of his needs."

We cross the hall to his room and the staff is already waiting for us." Good morning, ladies. Thank you for meeting me here today. This is Nashville. She's my father's new nurse and she'll be working on your scheduling needs for you. You'll report to her any issues that may arise with my father. She has my complete trust, so she's your new boss."

There are six staff members, and I pay them well. They rotate out twenty-four seven. They all seem very receptive to Nashville. She wins them over easily with her southern accent. I stand back and watch her in action. She's beautiful and sexy as hell. Those high heel shoes on her are killing me. I liked the cowboy boots, but what she does to those heels should be illegal. My heart is racing visualizing removing them from her. My libido is in overdrive.

"We have worked out what minor issues they have. I'd really like to do a complete assessment on your father."

"Okay, I have some work I need to do in my

office. Why don't you meet me down there when you're all done?"

I CALL Sam to let him know that Fred will be picking him and Claire up at five, then he'll come back and pick me up.

"Are you bringing Nashville with you?" he asks.

"I had not planned on it." I'd really like to keep as much information away from her as possible. She knows Sam, but she has no idea the role I play in their lives, or how I got involved with them.

"You should bring her."

"I'm not bringing her Sam. Let it go."

"Then why don't you take her out on a date afterward?"

I don't reply.

"Okay, okay," he says. "I just want you to have a little fun."

"I'm going to have fun watching you graduate tonight. I'm so proud of you. Have you thought any more about college?"

"Actually, I have. I've looked into Main Sail. It is a good computer graphic college. I can take most of my classes online, but I really want to get out and meet some people my age. Maybe even meet some pretty little girl from Tennessee."

"You don't give up do you?"

"I learned from the best. Mister control freak."

"I'll see you and your mom later." I hang up before he can rip on me anymore and return to the pile of papers on my desk.

I RECENTLY EXPANDED my company to design planes and boats, and we have a product launch next week. The expansion is the biggest endeavor I've taken on since I gained control of the company. I hired the best designers from all over the world. The launch will be at the Royal Hotel downtown Seattle next Saturday. I wonder if I should ask Nashville to be my guest. Lisa has been my date at the last few events, but I like the thought of Nashville being my side.

I'm totally absorbed in my work, so I jump when Nashville storms into my office." August, I need to talk you about Tom."

CHAPTER SEVEN

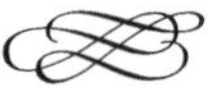

NASH

After everyone but the aide on duty left, I meticulously read all the physicians' reports on Tom. His stroke left him flaccid on the right side of his body. He has no muscle movement at all in his right arm or leg. He gets a lot more personal attention than your average stroke patient: regular physical therapy so his muscle atrophy is minimal and he has no contractures of his hand or limbs, and he's turned regularly so his skin looks good. He's fed high nutrient calories through a feeding tube in his abdomen. He voids in a brief and as adequate output.

I spoke with him as I assessed him. Everything in the reports said that he's unresponsive, so why'd I catch him following me with his eyes? I believe he's more responsive everyone thinks. He didn't follow any commands, but I know I caught him watching me. He's in there. Suddenly, my job has new meaning. I'm determined to bring him out.

I don't mean to startle August when I bust into his office, but he jumps. I hope he's not annoyed with me. As he shuffles his papers, I try to think of where to begin.

"I'd like to spend a few hours a day alone working with your father. I really think I can improve things for him." I don't want to give August any false hope so I don't expand on what I think the possibilities could be.

"You're the boss. Make it happen." He seems so nonchalant.

I can't even tell him how excited I am." I'd like to get started sooner than we planned. My last shift at the hospital is Tuesday. I could move in here on Wednesday. If that's okay with you?"

He smiles, and it's beautiful. "Absolutely."

My mind goes back to that kiss. I wasn't misreading him. He does like me. I could feel the sexual energy literally vibrating off of him.

"Do you have plans Saturday?" he asks.

"I was thinking about visiting my parents. Why what's up?"

"I have this... this thing... on Saturday. I was wondering if you'd accompany me?"

I get the feeling that "this thing" is something big." What thing?"

"I'm launching a new branch of my company. The party is in Seattle Saturday night. It's black tie." He suddenly looks shy. "I'd love to have you by my side."

"I don't know. I've never been to a fancy party like that. I wouldn't know how to act. I definitely don't have anything to wear." I bite the inside of my lip.

"Why would you want to act any other way than who you are? You're a little feisty at times, and you have a potty mouth, but other than that you're charming."

I smile at his description of me." I'm not sure all of that was a compliment, but I'll take it as one. I guess once I get settled here on Wednesday I could go shopping for a dress."

"I'll have Fred, my driver, bring you to the airport Saturday. He'll fly with you on my private plane, then he can drive you to the hotel."

"You have a private plane?"

"I own the private airport too." He says this as if everyone has their own plane and airport.

He's not just rich. He's uber rich. I've always wanted a simple life. A small house on a ranch, away from everything. My goals are not big. I like him, but I'd never fit in his world.

"Are you okay?" He's frowning at me.

"You and your money are a little overwhelming."

He pulls me from the chair into his arms." I may be overwhelming, but you're intoxicating to me." He kisses me lightly this time.

"I thought you didn't date your employees?"

"Well, I could fire you before you start, or I could make an exception for you."

"I like the exception part, but honestly August, you scare me."

"I scare you?"

"This." I wave my hand around." You and your planes and cars and your mansion of a house. You're so out of my league."

He grabs me and kisses me again. Deeper this time." I'm just a guy. The rest doesn't mean anything. Besides, you scare the hell out of me too." He whispers the last part.

"I scare you?" I don't think I've ever scared anyone.

"You scare me when you take my breath away."

He kisses me again. "You scare me when you infuriate me when you argue with me." And again.

"You scare the fuck out of me when you wear those damn cowboy boots and it makes me hard." The kiss deepens and I can feel how turned on he is. He picks me up and wraps my legs around his waist, and sets me on the desk. He kisses a path down my neck to the top of my breast. I feel the wetness between my thighs. He reaches behind me and flings everything off his desk, just like in the movies. I giggle and he hushes me with his mouth.

"Now's not the time for laughter, Nash." He's so serious. It's hot but intimidating.

A shrill noise pierces the moment. It's either the burglar alarm or the fire alarm.

"Damn it." He says and helps me off the desk. We run into the kitchen.

Stella is speaking in Italian and waving an oven mitt. She's coughing from the smoke billowing from the stovetop. August grabs a fire extinguisher from under the bar and puts out the flame.

"I'm sorry, Mr. Rylan. I only stepped away for a minute." Stella is crying.

She's gripping her arm.

"Did you burn yourself?" I ask.

She winces and nods.

"August," I say, "I saw a medical bag in your dad's room. Get it for me, please."

He runs to the stairs.

"Sit down," I say to Stella. "Let me take care of you."

"He's going to be so mad." She whimpers.

"Don't be silly. It was an accident." I wonder if he has been angry with her before. Maybe he has a temper and I haven't seen it yet.

"Here you go." August has returned with the bag.

"I'm so sorry, Mr. Rylan. I will pay for any damages."

"Don't be ridiculous, Stella. I just want to make sure you are okay. This stuff can be replaced." He rubs her shoulders.

He seems honest in his response to her. I don't think he can fake that. I find the burn cream and rub it on her arm and then wrap it with gauze." You'll want to redress this tomorrow and apply more cream. It should keep it from blistering. You're lucky it isn't any worse." I turn to August." While I have this medical bag out, why don't you let me remove your stitches?"

He places his hand in mine and smiles.

* * *

I'm under his scrutiny as I carefully remove each stitch. His face is so close I can feel his breath on my face.

"There. All done," I say." It looks really good. Does it still hurt?"

"No, not at all." He examines it." Now I can actually shave." He rubs his chin.

I pout at him." I really like your scruffy face." It's funny how he sometimes intimidates me, and sometimes I really get a kick out of sassing him.

"Do you now?"

Stella interrupts our moment again." I'm sorry, sir, but you asked me to keep you on schedule today. If you don't hurry up, you're going to be late for Sam's graduation."

He closes his eyes tight like he is trying to switch gears." Thank you, Stella. Call someone to repair the kitchen, please. And please, don't worry about it."

"Yes, sir," Stella says, and I can hear the relief in her voice.

"It's okay," I say. "I need to get going anyway. I promised Anna a girls' night out." I grab my purse and August follows me to the door. He calls Fred and asks him to meet me out front. As we reach the front door, he has a crease in his forehead.

"What are you worried about?" I ask him as I rub the crease between his brow.

"Will you ladies be drinking tonight?"

"I'm sure we will."

"Let me have Fred be your designated driver."

"That's not necessary. We'll take an Uber. Besides, Fred is tied up with you and Sam tonight."

"I can drive the Jag. I'd rather know you two be safe." Before I can argue with him, he has Fred back on the phone. He gives Fred the new plan: to be my chauffeur. Poor Fred, August runs him everywhere.

Fred is already parked in the driveway. August opens the limo's back door." Give me your phone."

I dig it out of my purse and decide not to argue with him. He takes it and programs in a number." This is Fred's number. Call him anytime you need him." Fred nods in agreement and August kisses my cheek." He will stay close to you tonight. Have fun, but not too much fun."

I climb into the limo and August shuts the door. Fred eases out of the driveway through the front gates.

"I'm sorry Fred. You don't have to be at my beck-oned call."

He smiles at me in the rearview mirror." It's my job miss. Wherever Mr. Rylan wants to send me, I go."

"Is he always so bossy and controlling?"

He laughs, "Yes. Yes, he is."

I don't think I like the idea of being bossed around, this is something we are going to have to discuss outside of our employee-employer relationship. I do like how he took control when we were in his office. When he kissed me and hushed me at the same time it turned me on. No doubt. I scowl. So I like him to be in charge, but not too much in charge.

My last boyfriend, in college, had no idea what he was doing during sex. It was all about his pleasure, not mine. I get the feeling that August knows how to please a woman. Everything about his is commanding. I want him to touch me. And I want to touch him back.

I think about his hard body next to mine. His arms and shoulders are well defined. I would love to see him completely naked. I'm getting wet just thinking about him. I need to stop.

I THANK Fred for driving me and rush into the apartment. I can't wait to tell Anna about the kiss, and how close we were to having sex. I know I signed a nondisclosure with him about his father and I'll have to honor that, but he didn't say I couldn't talk about him with my best friend.

I tell her all about it as we get ready for our girls' night out.

"I told you he liked you!" she squeals." I can't believe he is flying you in his personal plane to Seattle. I have always wanted to visit that town. I've heard its so cool. I'm so jealous."

"Don't be jealous. I'm scared to death. I don't know anything about fancy parties." I plop down on the bed.

"Just be yourself. Don't let people with money intimidate you!We'll have fun dress shopping." She's so excited." But for now, let's get you in something really hot for our night out. I want to dance and pick up men. If we show a little bit of that cleavage of yours, men will be falling over to dance with us." She hands me a low-cut, form-fitting gold dress.

"I thought we were going line dancing?"

"We are. And we're going to look hotter than hell while we're doing it."

* * *

The bar is packed with cowboys wearing tight jeans. Anna is dancing a jig at the prospects. My mind keeps wandering back to city boy with a scruffy looking face. For the first time in my life, cowboys don't interest me.

We sit at the bar and order our first round of drinks. After that, the drinks just show up, one after another.

"My favorite song!" Anna drags me onto the dance floor. We line dance to the next five songs, surrounded by hot sweaty male bodies.

"I need some water!" I yell to Anna over the music. She waves me off and continues dancing.

I push through the crowd toward the bar and see a familiar face. Fred is at the end of the bar, talking on the phone. That doesn't sit well with me. I was supposed to call him when we were ready to leave. I finish my water and sip at another drink, this one from a blonde guy in a tight tee-shirt who can't stop staring at my breasts. I'm starting to feel a little tipsy. Anna grabs my shoulder, trying to pull me onto the dance floor again.

By one in the morning, I'm really lightheaded. Anna is making out in the back of the bar with some dude. I clumsily make my way over to her. "It's time to go," I say, and the words sound garbled in my own ears.

She briefly disconnects her lips from the cowboy's mouth." I have a ride home." She laughs and runs a hand down his chest.

I walk into the bathroom to splash water on my face. I dig out my phone and call Fred." Can I still have a ride home? I know it's late."

"Your ride is outside the bar."

"Thank you so much."

The crowd is still rocking, so it takes me a while to get to the door. I walk outside, but I don't see the limo. Instead, I see the Jaguar. The windows are so black I can't see inside, but my heart starts beating faster at the thought that August must be inside. The driver's side door opens and he steps out, wearing a perfectly tailored suit. I wonder if there is enough room in that Jag to fuck him.

He puts an arm around my waist." Why are you here?" I scowl at him.

"Because I want to be." He steers me into the passenger seat, and buckles me in, like the last time.

"Did you have Fred watching us?"

"Yes. I wanted him there in case things got out of hand." He puts the car in gear." Here I brought you a coffee." He hands it to me. "I want you sober by the time I get you home."

There goes that sexual energy rolling off of him again. I press my legs together to stifle the throb between them.

"I take it Anna won't be coming home tonight?"

I shake my head and drink my coffee. I have a feeling that I'm indeed going to want to be sober for what he has in mind.

I HAND him the key and he unlocks the apartment. He pushes me inside, shuts the door and presses my body up against it.

"Do you have any fucking idea how much I want you right now?" He rubs his hand at the hem of my dress." The thought of you dancing with all those men in these damn boots of yours." He breathes into my mouth. His hand blazes a trail down my leg and I want to combust. Body heat radiates off him.

"Tell me what it is you want, Nash." He growls against that spot just below my ear. He spins me around and pins my palms to the door. I feel his hard length against my ass as his kisses trail down my neck. I break his grasp on my hands and turn around to kiss him. My greedy hands find his belt.

"I want you." I rub my hand down his rock hard cock. "I want this too."

His eyes widen and he picks me up." Which room is yours?"

"The one on the left." I barely get the words out before his mouth is on mine again. As he is carrying me, my itchy fingers find the buttons on his shirt. I feel my feet hit the ground as my hands find his ripped abs. I bite his nipple.

I loosen his belt and tug at his pants until he springs free. I wrap my hands around him and he sucks in a deep breath. This might be the only time I have control over this man. I'm going to relish in it.

I get on my knees and I taste him. I'm so wet with a hunger for him. I start at the tip and take him in shallow at first. Soft and slow. I listen to his strained breathing. I apply pressure and take him deeper in my mouth. He grabs my hair, and pulls, and mutters a few curse words. As he pops free of my mouth he pulls me to my feet.

"Enough. My turn to take what I want." He pushes me back on the bed and pulls off my boots." These, we'll use another day. I can't wait to get my fucking hands on you." He stares at me with stormy eyes.

Sweet Jesus, let the storm come down.

He strips me of my panties and then my dress. He coaxes my legs apart. I'm completely exposed to him. I blush when he looks at me. He's like a starving man who suddenly finds himself at a feast as if he can't decide where to begin satiating himself. He licks my clit, and I feel it vibrate. I try to close my legs, but he won't allow it. He sucks at me." You taste sweet," he mutters. His words and his mouth rock me to my core. He keeps licking and teasing me until I can take no more.

My eagerness for him is tenfold, despite my orgasm. I cannot wait to take him inside of me. He grabs his pants and takes a condom from his pocket. His cock throbs as he rolls it onto him.

The intensity of in his eyes has me on the verge of another orgasm." You're wet and ready for me." He runs his hand over my clit.

"Yes,"I whisper into his shoulder.

His body covers me, and I'm panting. I hitch my leg over the tight muscles of his thighs, landing on his equally tight ass. I wiggle beneath him, trying to coax him into me. He grabs my hips and kisses me. I can taste myself on his tongue. He slips just the tip of his cock into me.

He's in complete control of my body. My need for him to be inside me is blinding. He suddenly thrusts, deep, and I let out a cry of pleasure against his mouth. I relish the feeling of fullness of him. He drives into me and my body achingly, deliciously accommodates him.

"You're so fucking tight." He rotates his hips and hits that spot inside of me that sets me on the edge of another orgasm. He senses it and holds back for a moment. His pause staves off my orgasm.

He slowly starts again, thrusting in and out of me. His strokes are calculated. Thrust, pause, thrust. My release is so close. His mouth covers mine again, and it's like he's devouring me.

"August, please." I don't recognize my own begging voice. I've never felt such pleasure.

"Trust me, baby." He whispers. He grabs my ass and drives deeper. I scream out his name again. He touches parts of me that have never been touched. I grip his shoulders as he thrusts hard again. I clutch his hair.

"Fuck, baby. Come for me now."

My body clenches around him as my orgasm

ravishes my body. He lets out a roar and pulses inside me.

Our breathing slows and I collapse against him. Our bodies are tangled together. I softly kiss his shoulder and grin up at him.

He smiles back." Something humorous?"

"Not at all. I just didn't know sex could feel that good." I rest my cheek on his shoulder and hum in satisfaction. He pulls me close and squeezes me.

"I need to go take this damn condom off." He pushes me back onto the bed and stands. I want to follow him but I don't think my legs will work. I watch his fine ass and muscular thighs. I'm glad I didn't move. I've never seen such a finely sculpted man. I shiver. He's swept through my life like a tornado and has obliterated my senses.

I WAKE up to light peering through my blinds. For a moment, I think last night was a dream until I roll over and see August sleeping on his belly. He's beautiful, and his just fucked hair has my fingers itching to run my fingers through it again. His body is so relaxed. As my hand goes toward his back, his eyes pop open and he lifts his head.

"Hey, blue eyes." His voice is gravely.

I splay my hand on his back." Hey, yourself." I kiss his shoulder blade." I have to go to work."

He rolls over and pins his body to mine." Quit today, and we can have a repeat of last night. Or even better." He kisses my chin.

I laugh. "It gets even better? I won't survive."

"Spend the day with me in bed."

"As tempting as that sounds, I can't. We're already shorthanded at work." I untangle my body from his. He lays there and watches me as I unabashedly saunter to the bathroom, hoping to tempt him into the shower. I leave the door open and turn on the water. I wait until it's warm, and as I walk in, he comes in behind me.

Needless to say, I am going to enjoy being late for work.

CHAPTER EIGHT

AUGUST

I've been unfocused since I stepped out of Nashville's shower on Sunday. I still have hints of her scent on me, even though I've been stuck in Seattle all week preparing for the launch party. I thought once would be enough, but I want her even more. She's been so busy at work she's been sending monosyllabic responses to my texts. It's driving me batshit crazy.

She moves in today and I'm stuck here, in Seattle, in this office. Last Sunday, while she was getting ready for work, I rummaged through her closet to see what size dress she wears. I ordered her a navy blue gown for the party. I laid it on her bed so that she'll see it as soon as she gets to the house. I've envisioned her in it several times today. I couldn't sit in my office with a raging hard on, so I went to the gym in my building and worked out. All that did was feed my endorphins and I ended up in a cold shower. Thank god that worked, or I was going to have to give myself a hand job before my meeting with a new client.

The meeting goes off without a hitch, and the day flies by, until Bob, one of my financial advisors calls me. He tells me that the family that had blamed my father for their son's death, in the second car accident, are snooping around again.

As far as anyone knows, my father himself is dead. Only my staff knows he's lingering in a vegetative state, and I want to keep it that way. I refuse to continue to pay for my father's sins. I need to protect what I've built. Besides, before my mom died, I loved my dad. He was a good man, but he blamed me for her death. I can still hear him drunkenly yelling through my bedroom door, "If you weren't such a pain in the ass crybaby, maybe your mother would still be here." Then there were the beatings, of course, As I got older, I knew that he was to blame for her death. He was the one drinking and driving the car. I was just a scared kid. At least my rational mind knew that. No matter how old you get, the idea that one of your parents, and in my case, my only remaining parent, hates you, does some damage.

They were celebrating their ten-year anniversary the night she died. I was at a sleepover with a classmate and we got in a fight over something. I don't even recall what it was. His mom called my parents to come pick me up. They had both had a few drinks, so they didn't use good judgment getting behind the wheel. So I lived with that guilt my whole life: the sleepover fight, and my crying in the car and distracting my dad. The second crash, however, I had nothing to do with, and I refuse to feel guilty about it.

"I'll have our security team on alert," I say. "Thank you for letting me know."

I pull out my phone and punch in speed dial for Wayne. I update him on the new information and have him beef up security." I want a man at the front gate of my house. Just as an extra precaution."

"Consider it done, sir," says Wayne.

I hang up. I punch in Nashville's number. I need to let her know, but it's really just an excuse to hear her voice.

"Hey. I just arrived at your house," she says.

"Good, I'm glad you'll be living there. I wanted you to know that there will be a security guard at the front gate. I'll have you cleared before he even starts."

"Did something happen?" She sounds alarmed.

"No, nothing to concern yourself about. I miss you." I want to change the subject, and it's not a lie.

She is quiet.

"Is something wrong?" I ask.

"No.... it's..... just, well I think we got involved a little too quickly."

"Are you having regrets?"

"I don't regret anything we have done to each other. I rather enjoyed myself, it's just a little complicated for me working for you. We need to have some boundaries."

I don't think I can have boundaries where she's concerned." We'll work it out. I enjoy spending time with you, Nash. We can go a little slower if you like." I have no intention of slowing down what is between us. I've never felt this way, and I want to explore it even more.

"Thanks for saying that, I really want to get settled here and start working with your father right away. I'm anxious to see what kind of progress I can make with him."

I'm not really interested in his progress. I take care of him out of loyalty, nothing else. I hate what he has done and who he had become. There are days I just wish him dead. I'm sure if I said these words out loud, it would make me a monster." Don't get your hopes up too much Nash, he has been this way for a while. Work on getting settled in and making yourself at home. If you need anything, please let Stella know."

"I have everything I need. Quit worrying about me. I can take care of myself."

"Did you get the email with the agenda on Saturday?"

"Are you sure you want me to go? I don't want to hinder you at the party and I'm not so sure about fitting in with everyone." She says.

"I'm absolutely positive that I want you on my arm. I'll be honored to show you off." I reassure her.

"Okay," she says, "I'll see you on Saturday."

* * *

My panel of experts is wrapping up their final plans for the launch when Margaret walks in and whispers in my ear.

"You have a phone call, sir."

"Take a number. I'll call back."

"I think you might want to take it. The man is very insistent. He says if you don't talk to him he'll talk to a reporter."

"Thank you for all of your hard work ladies and gentlemen. I have a pressing issue I need to address." I follow Margaret out.

"I'm so sorry I interrupted your meeting."

"You did the right thing, Margaret. I'll take it in my office." I close the office door and my desk phone rings. I call Wayne on my cell.

"I need you to track the call on line three. "I hang up and take the incoming call. "Hello?"

An unwavering male voice responds." Is this August Rylan?"

"Yes. Who's this?" I lean back into my chair.

"My name isn't important, but you need to listen very carefully. I'm going to ruin you. Your father took something from me and never paid the price for it. You'll pay for his sins. I think you're hiding something and when I find out what it is, I'll destroy you." The phone line goes dead.

Wayne dials in as soon as the call ends." He wasn't on long enough sir for me to trace him. I have already doubled security on the main floor, and I put a guard by the elevator on your floor, sir."

"I'm more concerned about my home."

"I'm on it, sir." He hangs up.

Shit. When is it ever going to end? Now I've drawn Nashville into this mess. This is why I've had no life. As soon as I let my guard down, this shit starts up again. If the accident would've been my father's fault, I would've handed them over every penny the man had left, but it wasn't. The twenty-eight-year-old man driving the truck was on his cell phone at the time he ran into my father, who was parked on the side of the road. When he struck my dad's car from behind, he lost control. His truck hit the railing on a small bridge. He plummeted over the edge into the water. Yes, he died, but my dad was passed out in his car. He never even knew what happened. He was drunk, but he was parked off the road. The man's family insisted that my dad's drunkenness played a key role in the accident, and he should pay. The court dismissed all charges against my father, but the family has been out for vengeance ever since. I thought if they believed he was dead, then they'd let it go. Evidently not. They want me to pay.

I need some air.

I take the stairs to the rooftop. I walk over to the railing and stare out into the city. I can see Pike's Market from here. There's always a crowd by the water. As much as I love this city, I would rather be in Utah. It is a different kind of beauty. It has a peacefulness that I can't find here.

I loosen my tie to release some of the forebodings that phone call brought with it. I wonder if I should call Nashville and cancel our plans. I should keep things on a professional level with her. The thought displeases me. I don't want to keep her at arm's length. I want her in my bed. Still, I don't want her any more involved in the secretive part of my life than she already is.

I call her with every intention of canceling until I hear that sweet southern drawl.

"Did you miss me so soon?" She teases as she answers.

I just can't do it." Yes."

She must sense my ache." Are you okay?"

"Yeah, I'm better now that I have heard your voice. It's just been a long rough day at work."

"MARGARET, I need a car. I have a meeting."

"I'll have a driver wait out front for you, but I don't recall a meeting on your schedule?"

She keeps close tabs on me." I don't need a driver. I just need a car. It's a last minute meeting. I forgot to tell you this morning."

"I'll take care of the car, but it's not like you to not update me."

I can't be angry with her for her concern, but I just need to get the hell out of here." You're right. I usually don't forget. But I did today. I need the car in ten minutes."

I FEEL a little unsteady when I park at the cemetery. The loneliness I feel here always depresses me, but I need to see her. I walk through the maze of headstones. For years, there was only a small memorial on her grave. With the first real money I made, I replaced it with a statue of an angel. Canailles surround her. She used to grow them in our yard. The smell of them reminds me of her. Our house never felt like home again after she died. Dad made life so difficult. I know he missed her and blamed me, but I missed her too.

"Hi, Mom. The flowers are looking nice. You'd love them. Dad is the same." I swallow hard." Sam just graduated from high school. You'd be proud of him, just like I am. And Claire...you two could've been good friends. She reminds me of you. Shit has stirred up with dad again. I should've expected it."

I sit on a bench I had placed by her gravesite." I have a beard now." I fumble for words." I cut my hand when I was mountain climbing with Sam and I met a girl. She has the most beautiful blue eyes. She's sweet and smart. She's not at all like other woman that I've met. You'd love her. I'm not sure what to do with her. My life has been so fucked up for years, I don't want her involved, but I feel like this woman could be my lifeline. The funny thing is, I just met her, but her soul draws me into her. She has a light about her that I can't explain. I need her, and I haven't needed anyone in years."

I ignore the phone vibrating in my pocket and I keep talking to her like she hears me. I used to do this every week, now I don't come but every couple of months. Some people would be surprised to see a grown man talking to a stone angel, especially a man who is as serious as I always am. But I don't care. Sometimes I just miss my mom.

CHAPTER NINE

NASH

He's not answering his phone. I wanted to thank him for the navy blue dress that he bought for me to wear Saturday, but at the same time, I wanted to scream at him for thinking he could dress me and spending the outrageous amount of money on the price tag.

I call Anna. "Are you still up for shopping?" I ask her.

"When and where?"

"Meet me at the mall."

"He bought you a dress that cost three thousand dollars?" Her mouth hangs open.

"Yes! Can you believe it?"

"Why are we here looking for a dress? I'm confused." She takes my elbow.

"I can't accept a gift like that. Besides, I don't want him dressing me. If I give him this, he will think that he can control me." I huff out." If he can't accept me for who I really am, then there's no point. I told you I didn't think I would fit into his world."

She pulls me over to a bench." What exactly it is you do for him?"

I have to remember the nondisclosure." I take care of his staff. Several of them are on some pretty heavy medications and they need to be monitored." I hate lying to her, I'm not very good at it.

She sees right through me." Yeah, right." She says sarcastically." Mr. Mysterious has his secrets and he has sucked you into them."

"I really can't discuss it with you. Or anyone else."

"I get it, but I'm worried about you. I at least hope he's amazing in bed," she says and laughs.

"Oh my god Anna, you have a one-track mind!" I laugh with her.

"Come on." She grabs my hand." Let's go find a dress that will rock his world."

* * *

Shopping was fun and we found the perfect dress. The perfect "me" dress. I can't wait to see the look on August's face when he sees me in it. I decide not to say anything about the other dress. I give it to Stella to return. She doesn't seem very happy about it, but she says she'll take care of it.

Today is my first day to spend some solo time with Tom. I decided there will be no aides with us from ten to four, Monday through Friday. Just me. Twice a week, I'll work with his physical therapists. I recommended occupational therapy, and a speech therapist to evaluate him. The physician taking care of him didn't really see the need, but he appeased me anyway.

"Good morning, Tom. I'm Nash. Do you remember me?" I watch him carefully for any signs of acknowledgment." I want to try some new things with you today." He doesn't respond in any way. It's disappointing, I admit. Maybe I just imagined responsiveness that first time I saw him. Or maybe I'm going to have to be patient.

I take his left hand in mine." Can you squeeze my hand?"

Nothing." Do you like television?" I pick up the

remote. The news is on. I switch channels several times and stop when I see Tom's head slightly turn. It is a woman playing the piano and singing. His eyes focus.

I knew it. I knew he's in there. I have to find something that will draw him out. I walk around to the foot of the bed to finish my daily assessment, and to my surprise, there's a stream of water coming from his left eye. He's still staring at the television. I grab a tissue.

I remember the piano in the great room and August telling me it was his mother's. It must remind him of when she played. I wipe away the tear with a tissue." You miss her after all this time." He blinks and then shuts his eyes.

I sit on the side of the bed and hold his hand again." Open your eyes, Tom,"I say softly. They remain closed." I know you can hear me. Open your eyes." I say a little more firmly.

His eyes open and he looks straight at me." Can you squeeze my hand?" I ask him again. He reaches up and touches my face. Oh my god, he is responsive. Why has no one seen this?

I'm elated." I can't wait to tell August!" He drops his hand and looks away.

"Tom, look at me." He has crawled back into his

shell and will not respond. He's hiding from August, but why? It gives me an idea. I take one of the unused journals that the aides use to document everything they do for Tom while they are taking care of him.

"Tom. I know you can move your hand and you can probably write. I'm going to lay this journal on your bed along with a pen. I need you to help me figure out what I can do for you. Tell me why you're hiding." He doesn't look at me." I'll leave the journal right here, just in case you change your mind."

I hover around for thirty minutes, fidgeting with things and tidying up even though nothing really needs tidying, but I get no further responses from him.

* * *

THE NEXT DAY, when I come in to relieve the aide, I notice the journal sitting on the nightstand." Why is this here?" I pick it up and ask her.

"When I came in last night it was on the floor." She answers.

I flip through the first couple of pages, but it's empty. Wishful thinking.

"Does he respond to you in any way?" I ask the aide.

"No, he never does. He's the same every day."

"Thank you for taking such good care of him." I walk her to the door and then turn around.

"Okay, Tom, time for me to check you out again." I start from his left side since he can't move the right side. As I pick up my stethoscope he grabs my hand lightly.

Rather than overreact, this time, I talk to him." There you are. Good morning," I say. His eyes find mine. He watches me as I assess him.

"Do you want me to find some music on the television for you?"

He nods slightly, so I reach for the remote and find a music channel. I stare at him as he watches the television. For the first time, I see a slight resemblance to August. They have the same dimpled chin and just underneath the gray, I see a smattering of black. The picture I saw of his mother on the piano, she had red hair. I look around the room and I don't see any pictures on the wall. That gives me another idea.

"I'll be right back." I run down the stairs, grab a picture off of the piano, and take it back to his room. When I show it to him, his tears start flowing again."

How about I set it on the shelf in front of you, so you can see her every day?" He nods again. Progress. I can't wait to tell August, but I don't dare say the words out loud again. He might tune me out.

At the end of my time with him, I lay the journal and the pen back on his bed." Just in case,"I say and smile at him." I'll be back Monday."

My flight to Seattle is amazing. The pilot lets me sit in the co-pilot seat, right beside him. He's friendly and nice, but I'm perplexed about how little personal information he knows about August. He's been flying him around for years.

Fred shuffles me off the plane and into a limo. My curiosity gets the better of me." Fred, what do you know about Tom and Sara?"

He glances back at me." Sara was killed in a car accident when August was eight. His father was never the same after her death."

"What about Tom and August after she died?"

He hesitates." Tom was rough on August."

He doesn't volunteer any more information so I decide I will wait. I'll ask August about it myself.

* * *

The city streets are bustling with people. Traffic is crazy, and I'm so thankful for Fred. He pulls up in front of this huge hotel. The architecture is beautiful. A red carpet lines the entryway. A bellhop opens my door as Fred takes my bags from the trunk. He hands them to the eager young man and gives him some cash." See to it that she makes it to her room."

I kind of expected August to meet me at the car." Where's August?" I ask Fred.

"He has some loose ends to tie up. He said to tell you he will meet you at the party at eight."

I glance at my watch that gives me about two hours to kill. I follow the bellhop to the massive elevators. He pushes the button for the top floor. I'm anxious as we go up. The doors open into a single hall with a heavy wooden door

"This is your floor, madam." He grabs my bags.

"The entire floor?"

"It's Mr. Rylan's penthouse suite. He left instructions for you on the table. Here's my card. When you're ready to go to the party, call me and I'll come get you." He opens the door and places my bags just inside the door.

The décor is all white with a breathtaking view

of the city. I see the famous Ferris wheel, the one that's in so many pictures of Seattle. I even have a glimpse of the Space Needle.

There's a note in the kitchen.

"I can't wait to see you in your dress. I hope you liked it. Just in case I forget to tell you, thank you for being by my side tonight. Make yourself at home. Order anything you like. There's a bottle of white wine in the refrigerator in case you're feeling a little nervous. Just be yourself, Nash.

I could use that wine. I hope he's not disappointed when he sees me in the dress I bought instead of the one he gave me.

The shower is bigger than the kitchen at my apartment. I take my dear sweet time shaving all my bits. I towel off and decide to tackle my hair first. Someone knocks, so I don the luxurious white robe hanging in the bathroom and head for the door. I peek through the peephole and there's a stunning looking woman holding several bags. Is she looking for August? A twinge of jealousy hits me. I tentatively open the door.

"May I help you?"

She brushes by me." I'm here to do your hair and makeup." She says it like I should've been expecting her.

"I don't understand?"

"August had me clear my schedule so that I could help you get ready for the party." She sets her bags down.

"Thank you, but I don't need your help." I cross my arms, anger bubbling up.

"He said you might say that, but I'm supposed to stand my ground. He said if I left without doing my job, I'll be fired."

That controlling son of a bitch. I have a mind to not even go to the party. The woman starts fidgeting.

"Please," she says, and she suddenly looks kind of pitiful. "I really like my job."

I can't be angry with her. This is all on August. I relent and show her to the bathroom.

I hate to admit it, but she is awesome. I don't even recognize myself in the mirror. The makeup is a bit much for me, but my hair looks amazing. It is so shiny and soft. She pulled it into a high loose bun. Locks of it fall around my face.

"Thank you so much." I reach for my wallet to tip her. She stops me.

"Mr. Rylan has already taken care of that," she says gently.

Of course, he has. I thank her again and walk her out.

I have about thirty minutes left before I need to leave. I look back in the mirror and wipe some of the excess makeup off my face. Much better.

My dress is black with silver beads around the low cut neckline and around the hem. It is long with a slit up the side. I slide on the matching bra and garter with silky hose. I paired it with strappy high heels that wrap around my ankles. I feel so tall and sexy. I put on silver dangling earrings that Anna insisted would be perfect with the outfit. I spent way too much, but I wanted to look nice for August. The dress he bought me was way too elegant. I would've been fidgeting all night. This is simple but very pretty and a little sexy. Anna assured me that it would be perfect for the party.

I find my black clutch and put my lipstick inside along with my wallet. I retrieve the card the bellhop left and dial his number.

I wait outside the elevator doors, fully expecting the bellhop. When the doors open, I am frozen in place by the sight of the man leaning casually against the elevator walls. August straightens and saunters toward me. His eyes are all over my body. He walks a circle around me and I can feel the heat radiating off of him.

When he's behind me he slips his arm around

my waist." This is not the dress I bought for you." He says so close to my ear that he has given me goose bumps.

He turns me toward him." You don't like it?"

He glances at my cleavage and carnal appreciation sweeps over his face." You're going to fucking kill me in this dress." He kisses me, and I'm breathless when he pulls away.

"You look handsome in your tux." I manage to mutter.

"I'm tempted to cancel the party and keep you to myself, but I really want to show you off." He kisses me again.

"We could be a little late." I smile up at him.

He growls." Tempting, but divesting you of this dress will have to wait. We have a full house of people waiting on us."

I kiss him this time." Maybe we could locate the coat closet while we're down there."

"I like the way you think." He smacks my ass.

He pulls me into the elevator and presses me against the wall. I can feel his erection between us. I'll have marks on my neck from his beard." My neck is going to be red."

"Good. It will mark you as mine." He places his hand between my legs." I can't wait to make your skin red here." He inserts a finger into me, then sticks it in his mouth.

I gape at him. I want to dislike what he just did, but it was so damn hot. There's throbbing between my legs. The elevator doors open. How am I supposed to walk out of here after what he just did to me?

My first step falters. He catches me and laughs. I regain my composure and straighten my shoulders." You're not one bit funny."

He takes my hand and walks me out.

The gala room is decorated in all white. Elegant chandeliers cover the ceiling. Flowers and candles add to the glamor and sophistication. I suddenly feel very uncomfortable. August's choice of a dress would have been more fitting. I feel underdressed in comparison to the women around me. Everyone, male and female, watches August pass by. Several of the women can't resist touching him, or kissing his cheek. He grips my hand as we walk to the front table. A woman with long black hair stops him and whispers something in his ear. He smiles but doesn't say anything back to her. She slides a card into his pocket.

He introduces me to a few people, but he keeps me snuggly tucked into his side as he talks. A small orchestra plays softly in the background as he pulls out my chair. I can't help but fidget. Suddenly, I fully understand the phrase "a fish out of water."

August places his hand on my thigh and leans into me." Stop squirming. You look absolutely stunning." I feign a smile at him and try to relax.

The crackle of a mic behind me startles me.

"Relax, Nash," he whispers.

The gentleman behind the mic begins his speech." I would like to thank August Rylan for making tonight happen." He goes on to talk about Rylan Designs and all of its accomplishments this year, and their plans for the future. Then he gets to the interesting parts.

"Mr. Rylan contributes annually to scholarships for nurses. Every year, he personally selects four deserving students for a scholarship. Not only does he pay for their schooling, he pays each of them a salary as long as they are in school. And his company provides each of them with a vehicle.

August holds my hand under the table." I hate this part. I wish they'd just move on."

"You should be proud. They are," I whisper.

"Not only does he contribute to these bright young people. He supports Mothers Against Drunk Driving all over the country. He recently finished building a state of the art building for an alcohol abuse rehab center, right here in Seattle. He has four additional sites slated to open later this year in different parts of the country."

I glance at August and he looks embarrassed. He really is a good person, so why doesn't he want people to know? He stands up and takes the mic from the presenter." That's enough about me." He turns to the crowd and smiles. He thanks all of his employees for all of their accomplishments. He takes nothing for himself. It's all about the people that work for him.

When he's done applaud rolls around the room. He sits beside me again and kisses my cheek. I notice sneers and rolling eyes from other women around me. I look at those beautiful woman, and wonder why me?

A waiter sets down a silver rimmed plate in front of us." You're thinking too much." August rubs the crease in my brow." Stop it."

After we eat the band starts playing and couples wander onto the dance floor.

August asks me to dance, so I take his hand and follow him. His arms around me finally make me relax. We move around the floor easily, and I almost forget there are other people here. Our eyes are locked on each other. His smile is beautiful. The song slows and I feel a hand on my shoulder. It's the woman with the long black hair. The one who slipped the card in his pocket." Would you mind if I dance with the man of the hour?" she asks.

"My dance card is full tonight," August tells her and sweeps me away from her. Her jealous eyes pierce me.

When the song finishes, August puts his arm around my waist and ushers me through the crowd to a balcony. He asks the people that are enjoying the view to give us a minute. They do as he asks and he shuts the doors behind them.

His walks toward me, and I'm reminded of a tiger on the prowl. His muscles flex through his tux. I lick my lips. I know his intent. He pushes me in a corner out of the view of the door. His lips are on mine, and he hikes my leg over his hip.

"You are fucking beautiful. Don't ever doubt yourself in front of me again."

I taste his anger at me with each stroke of his tongue. One hand is holding the back of my neck. His other hand finds its way inside my dress and caresses my breast. My nipples are hard. I find his zipper and release him. He lets go long enough to put a condom on his daunting length. His breath releases in a hiss as he thrust into my slick folds. He goes so deep that I gasp. He doesn't stop. He trusts several more times and then changes his position.

You.

Are.

Fucking.

Beautiful.

He says with each thrust. His words send me into a seemingly endless orgasm, and that in turn sends him off the edge.

We stayed connected until our breathing slows. This was a different type of sex for me. I almost felt like I was being punished. If that's the case, he can punish me anytime.

"Are you okay?" He asks as he kisses me.

"I like your brand of sex. I've never been with anyone like you." I kiss him lightly." Were you mad at me?" I whisper.

"Yes. I don't ever want you to doubt yourself."

"What happened to taking it a little slower?"

"Fuck slower. You drive me crazy. I'm angry at you for not wearing the dress I bought you." He kisses me again." But I'm also glad you are in this one."

"It was too much August. Not just the cost, it just wasn't me. I don't want you buying my clothes. I don't want you to make me into something that I'm not. Do you understand?"

"I'll try to understand."

"Thank you." I shiver.

"Are you cold, baby?"

"A little."

He pulls out of me and disposes of the condom in his pocket. He removes his tux jacket and drapes it around me." I think we should both hit the restroom to clean up." He takes my hand and leads me inside. Woman watch as we move through the room. Surprisingly, I'm not embarrassed at all. I hold my chin up high as to if to say, *yes, ladies he's mine and you can't have him.*

I finish up in the bathroom and wash my hands. I wrap his jacket around me and put my hand in the pockets. I feel the card that woman placed in his pocket. I pull it out. It has a club name on it. *Discreet Sexual Encounters.* It has a time and date filled out on it. She signed it, "I can't wait to meet up with you again."

I feel all the blood drain from my face. He belongs to a sex club, and he has been with that woman. I run back into the bathroom stall because I'm afraid I'll throw up. What the hell have I gotten myself into? I'm so stupid to think this rich hot man would just be a nice guy. Shit. I have to get out of here.

I wash my face and head for the door. I stand outside until I see a glimpse of August. His back is to me, and he is talking to a couple. This might be my only chance to get out of here without him seeing me. I walk along the outside wall until I make it out of the ballroom, and then I'm all but running in my high heel shoes. I'd give anything to have my boots on right about now. I make it to the elevator and the bellhop recognizes me and lets me in. He tries to make small talk, but I remain quiet. The elevator ride to the top seems to take forever.

I rush out with my key in my hand. I change into jeans and a t-shirt and tennis shoes. I pack my bags and head to the door. I have no idea where I am going or how I am going to get there, I just know I need to leave. I turn the doorknob, and August is standing on the other side of the door.

CHAPTER TEN

AUGUST

"Her bags are in her hands." Why are leaving?" It makes no sense to me. I thought we were having a great time.

"I don't belong here."

I take her shoulders and walk her backward into the suite. "I thought we just dealt with this. I don't understand. I was frantic when the bellhop called me and told me you looked upset. What happened?" I try to touch her but she steps away. I'm at a loss. A few minutes ago I had her in my arms and now she won't even let me touch her.

She puts her bags down and walks over to my tux jacket. She reaches in and pulls out a card and hands it to me.

"Where did you get this?" I ask.

"That woman with the long black hair that tried to cut in on our dance put it in your pocket."

"Fuck."

"Exactly," she says and laughs. "A lot of fucking."

"I've told you to watch your mouth." I rake my hands through my hair." It's not what you think."

"It looks pretty clear to me!"

"Please sit down so we can talk about this like adults."

She dramatically plops onto the couch.

I sit down beside her, but she scoots over to put distance between us.

"This was before you. I haven't been with this woman since the day you and I met."

"You expect me to believe that?"

"Look, you don't understand. Woman throw themselves at me all the time. I'm a wealthy bachelor. They don't see me. They see the money. I joined this private club because everyone that belongs is rich and in the same boat. There are no attachments and no strings, just sex."

She stares at me with those big blue eyes. She's fighting tears." I met you and all of that changed for me. I've never felt a connection with a woman until you. You don't care about my money. You see me." I reach for her hand and she lets me hold it.

"I think you only let me see what you want me to see," she says." There are truths that you cover up." She cocks her head at me." Why do you hide the good parts, like your scholarships and how you help strangers beat alcohol abuse?"

I release her hand and walk over to the dark view of the city. I feel her behind me." I'm not a good man, Nash."

She wraps her arms around my waist." I don't believe that. I heard all of the nice things your employees said about you. They respect you. I don't think they could respect a bad man. I don't think I could have fallen so hard and fast for a bad man."

I turn in her embrace at her words." I promise I've not been with anyone since I laid eyes on you. I want no other woman like I want you."

"I guess that is the real issue. I don't understand. Why me? You could have any one of those beautiful women. They're in the same class as you."

"You were the most beautiful woman in that room. You're real. Most of those women wouldn't know real if it hit them in the face. I can't impress you with my money. I buy you something and you send it back."

"I don't want things from you August. I just want you. I want your heart."

"All of this comes with me."

"And all the simple things come with me. So, we either learn to compromise or walk away." She pulls out of my arms and I pull her back.

"I don't want to walk away from you. You make me feel things I've never felt."

"Then I suggest you cancel your membership to your sex club."

"Easy enough. I don't have any desire to go."

"I don't expect you to have never been with any other woman before me. I just don't like it thrown in my face, and I hope I never see that woman again."

I kiss her softly." Wait. Does that mean you've been with other men before me?" I try to tease her to lighten the mood.

"I.... um...."

"I don't care who you've been with, but you're mine now. There will be no other man touching what is mine."

She smiles." Yours, huh?"

"Yes. Mine."

"I don't know...what do you have to offer me?" She asks as she walks toward the bedroom. She peels off her t-shirt and bra and throws it at me.

"Oh, baby. I am so glad you asked." I strip as I chase her into the room. She is standing naked on the far side of the king-sized bed. Her eyes are dilated and her nipples are begging for my mouth on them. She crawls across the bed and pulls me toward her.

"Show me what you got." I lay her down and part her legs. I've been imagining my beard between her legs, so now is my chance. I waste no time finding that spot that drives her wild. I love the sounds she makes as I lick and suck on her. Her fingers tighten in my hair. I feel her climbing to her climax. I love making her lose her control. Her breathing comes in pants, and I feel her tense. My fingers dig into her hips to hold her in place. Then I hear her scream out my name. It makes me so hard. I can't wait to plunge into her warmth.

She pulls me up to her and devours my mouth. I love that she gives as good as she gets." Please, I need to feel you inside me."

"I have a lot more to give you, baby." I kiss her.

"Save your magnificent skills for another time. I just want you to fuck me right now."

This is one time I don't mind her dirty little mouth." I have to get a condom."

"Don't you dare move. I'm on the pill."

"I think you just made my cock harder."

"Just shut the hell up and put it inside of me."

"You're a bossy little thing. I think it's time to

teach you who is in control of your orgasms." I roll her over and raise her behind in the air. Her head falls to the bed. I slowly enter her for the first time without a condom. She feels tight and glorious. I inch my way in and she arches her back. I place my hand in the center of her back and change her position slightly and then I slam into her. She lets out a pure scream of pleasure. I continue thrusting in and out of her until we both climax together, breathless.

* * *

My morning starts too early with the phone ringing. I ease out of bed. I don't want to wake Nash. She's sleeping naked on her belly. I find my pants and fish my phone out of the pocket.

"What?" I answer as I leave the bedroom suite.

It's Wayne, my security guru. "Sorry to call you so early, sir, but I finally got a lead on your threatening call the other day. It was the young man's father. We have pictures of him outside of the Royal Hotel last night."

"Shit. I don't want him anywhere near Nashville. Do you know where he is now?"

"No, sir. We didn't see the video until this morning. He was in a taxi. I'm trying to track down the Uber driver to find out where he picked him up."

I scrape my hands down my scratchy face." Okay, keep me posted."

"Is something wrong?" Nash is wrapped in a sheet, walking toward me.

I wrap my arms around her." Nothing for you to worry your pretty little head about." I kiss the top of her head.

"Mmmmm.... Your arms feel so good around me."

"I'll order us some breakfast and coffee."

"Sounds good. I'm going to get in the shower. Do you want to join me?" She pulls away.

"As tempting as you are, I really need to make some phone calls."

She drops her sheet and sashays her ass into the bedroom. She is going to kill me.

* * *

"WAKE UP SLEEPY HEAD. The plane has landed." I rub her arm. She slept the entire flight home.

"If someone wouldn't have kept me up all night trying to prove his skills, I wouldn't be so tired. And sore."

"Now you'll remember who owns you every time you move," I say, and she playfully swats me on the leg.

"You'll know who really has control when I show you my teeth." She chomps her teeth together.

"Remind me to not let you near my boy parts," I say and laugh.

When we get to the house, Stella has dinner waiting on us. We share an easy dinner together, talking and laughing.

"August, I really should go to my apartment tonight," she finally says.

"Please stay. I have to fly out again in the morning, so I won't see you until Tuesday night."

"Okay. Just let me call Anna and let her know I won't be home."

"Meet me on the couch when you're done. We can watch a movie." I kiss her and watch her fine ass leave the room. I have fallen for this woman so hard. I even debate skipping out on work tomorrow.

She bounces down on the couch beside me. I squeeze her knee. "How did it go with Anna?"

"She said she barely even missed me. She hooked

up with some of her friends and they partied all weekend." She cuddles next to me." What are we watching?"

"What do you prefer? I'm not really into television."

"Are you kidding me? Then why do you have a massive TV?"

"I had to have something fill the space on the wall," I say, laughing.

"In all my excitement this weekend, I forgot to tell you about your dad."

"I've already checked on him. Can we please not talk about him tonight?"

"Okay, but it's good news." She smiles up at me.

"Catch me up this week."

"I have an idea." She sits straight up." Let's go swimming in that big pool of yours. Or do you not really swim, you just needed to fill in that backyard of yours?"

"No swimsuits allowed." I get up and race her through the door. We both strip out of our clothes and dive in. I grab her and pull her under, and I kiss her. We both come up out of air and sputtering. When she catches her breath she starts laughing. God, I love her laugh. I love everything about her. She splashes me out of my thoughts.

"Come here." To my utter shock, she actually does as she is told. She wraps her legs around me and I just hold her. Neither one of us moves.

"Exactly how sore are you?" I say in her ear.

She laughs at me." You are insatiable."

"When it comes to you I can't get enough. I want my hands on you all the time."

"Our schedules aren't conducive for your hands to be on me all the time."

"I know, but now that you're living here, I can touch you every night."

"What are you doing this weekend?"

"I'm flying up to see my parents. I need to sort out exactly what their financial needs are so I can plan how much money to send them."

"Let me know. I'll get you the money they need."

"I appreciate the offer August, but the deal was I'd take the job so that *I* can help them. You can't just pay off their debt. This is my problem." She swims to the step.

"I consider anything that is your problem, my problem." I swim after her.

"You've been generous enough in my pay. For what I'm doing, I'm highly overpaid already."

"Do you have any idea how much money I have?"

"No, and I don't want to know. Your money has nothing to do with me." She points her finger at me." Find some charity to give your money to, not me."

I bite at her finger." You are one stubborn woman." I let it go for now and kiss her. I pick her up out of the water and carry her to the cabana and lay her on the chaise lounge chair. I know she complained of being sore, so I took the next hour and just worshiped her body and made love to her. When we were done, I curled her in my arms and carried her to my bed. No woman has ever slept in my bed, and now I never want this woman out of it. I watched her for hours as she blows out soft puffs of air, all curled into her pillow. How did she get to me so easily? She makes me lose control of my thoughts. I fall asleep happy for the first time in a long time.

CHAPTER ELEVEN

NASH

August was gone before I even dragged my lazy ass out of bed this morning. All this sex is wearing me out. I'm not complaining; I love how he makes me feel. I'm hopeful that he and I can work out our differences.

I meet Stella in the kitchen." Good morning, Stella."

She smiles sweetly at me." Good morning, Nash. Did you enjoy your weekend?"

"I did." I feel a little shy. She obviously knows what we've been up to.

"Mr. Rylan seemed very happy this morning. I think you put that smile on his face. It's good to see him look happy."

"Is August usually not happy?"

"Mr. Rylan is...let's say lonely. The only person he ever hangs out with is Sam."

I strum my fingers on the table." Has he always been a loner?"

She sits down on the barstool beside me and hands me a cup of coffee." Mr. Rylan has been on his own since his mother died. His aunt stepped in and helped him, but he had a lot to deal with at an early age. He was dealt a bad hand."

I don't want to overstep my bounds, but I want to get whatever information about him that I can. He isn't very forthcoming." Did he not get along with his father?"

"His father changed after his mother died. He drank a lot, and he had this awful temper that he had never had before. He blamed Mr. Rylan for his mother's death, and he took it out on him."

I gasp." What? How could he possibly blame a child for the accident?"

"His parents were out celebrating their anniversary and Mr. Rylan got in a fight with the boy he was staying with for the night and his parents had to come pick him up. They'd been drinking and were fighting over Mr. Rylan when the accident happened."

"Oh my god, poor August, he must have felt so

guilty. It wasn't his fault. He didn't get behind the wheel after drinking. That was a choice they made." I feel so bad for him.

"His father didn't see it that way. He blamed him every chance he got."

"So why does he take such good care of his father?"

"Because he is a loyal man and I think he always hoped his father would forgive him for something that wasn't even his fault. He remembers a man that was a good father up until the accident. I think he holds on to that."

That explains a lot about him. Maybe I can help him and his father mend a bridge. Tom is hiding from August for a reason. Maybe it's his own guilt. The information she has given me makes me more determined to draw Tom out.

"Thanks for talking with me. I hope I didn't cross a line with the nondisclosure."

"I love that boy like he's my own if I have to cross a line to help him, I will. I'm glad you're here. Just please don't break his heart. I think he has fallen hard for you. He has never brought a woman here before. That in itself says a lot."

I get up and hug her." Thank you, Stella." What she says makes me feel great, but also terrifies me.

* * *

The aide is leaving as I enter Tom's room." Any changes?"

"No. He's up in the chair. His physical therapy team just left. The speech therapist and occupational therapist are in there with him right now."

They're trying to work with him, but he's not responding to them at all. He has that blank stare on his face. They make their notes and leave. I read over what they've written. They both think it's a waste of time. I walk over to his chair and kneel in front of him.

"Good morning, Tom,"I say as I take his hand. His gaze meets mine. Why does he only respond to me? I don't get it. Most of these people have been working with him for a long time. Why don't they get anything out of him? I see his journal on the night-stand. I take it and flip through the first couple of pages again. Nothing. His eyes follow me.

"Why, Tom?" I plead with him. He opens his mouth like he is going to say something, but nothing comes out and he shuts his eyes hard.

I hand him the journal." Can you write it?"

He nods, but he doesn't write anything when I open the journal. He flips at the pages and gets frustrated and slaps at it. He makes a sound but I can't understand him.

"It's okay. We will get there. I'm not giving up on you."

I'm not sure, but I think the groan that comes out of his mouth might have been an expression of gratitude.

* * *

I KEEP my promise and I work with him every day. I actually had him tossing a ball with me. He still doesn't respond to anyone else. On Friday morning, I work with him on a puzzle. He slowly puts the pieces in place. There's a child in the puzzle. He points, and I clearly hear him say "Augie." I'm so excited about it. I can't wait to tell August, so I decide to call his office. I don't like calling his cell phone while he's at work, but this seems like as good a reason as any to call his office phone.

"Rylan Designs."

"Hi. May I speak to August?"

"I'm sorry, but Mr. Rylan doesn't come into the office on Fridays."

"What? You must be mistaken."

"Mr. Rylan never works on Fridays."

I hang up without saying goodbye. What the hell is he doing every Friday? He lied to me. The private sex club runs through my mind.

I call in the aide to cover my shift and I pack my bags. I call to change my flight home to an earlier flight. I run by the apartment and run into Anna.

"Hey girl, I've missed you around here." She hugs me.

"I've missed you too." Tears fill my eyes.

"Hey, what's wrong?" She leads me to the couch.

"Oh Anna, I think he is seeing someone else. I knew I wouldn't be enough for him." I cry on her shoulder.

"What makes you think that, sweetie?"

I tell her about calling his office, careful not to discuss Tom.

"Nash, if he hasn't been working on Fridays for a long time, maybe it's not what you think."

"What else could it be?" I sniff.

"I don't know, but I'm sure he can explain it."

"I don't care what his excuse is. He lied to me. There has to be trust in a relationship." I get up and head to my room.

"Aren't you curious?" She follows me.

"No. I'm pissed. I'm going to my parent's house

for the weekend. It will give me time to cool off." I throw some clean clothes into my suitcase.

"I'd go with you, but I'm scheduled to work tomorrow."

"It's okay. I'll be fine. I just need to get away from him right now. I was really falling for him. Just when I think he is a great guy, something bad comes up about him." As I say that my phone rings with his name flashing on it.

"Aren't you going to answer him?"

"No. I've nothing to say to him right now. I have a plane to catch."

By the time I park my car in the airport parking lot, August has blown up my phone at least ten times. I keep sending him to voicemail, and I don't want to listen to whatever he has to say. I turn it off and head for the terminal. I need to be away from him to gain some type of perspective.

The flight is only an hour long, but I fight back my tears the entire time. I catch a cab for the short ten-minute ride to my parent's farm.

"Mom. Dad," I call as I walk through the front door.

"Oh sweetheart, you're early. You should have called us. We would've picked you up." My mother engulfs me into a hug." Are you hungry?" Mom always tries to feed me." Your dad will be down in a minute. He was just cleaning up for dinner."

"I'm not really hungry. It's so good to see you." I hug her again and I hear my dad coming down the stairs.

"Hey, sweetheart." He looks happier than the last time I saw him.

"You look great." I hug him.

"I should look great now that the weight of the world has been lifted off my shoulders. Thanks to you."

"What do you mean? I came here this weekend so we could sit down and figure out how much money you need to keep things going."

We walk into the living room and sit down." All of that has been taking care of. I don't know how you did it so quickly, but our entire mortgage has been paid in full. There's even some extra money to make equipment repairs."

Did I just hear him right? August. Damn him. I get up and start pacing the floor and as I do, the tears start to flow.

"What's wrong?" My mother asks.

“I didn’t give you that money, the man I’ve been working for did it!”

They’re both speechless.” I started working for him because he was paying double what the hospital was paying me, and he has more money than sense. He’s a controlling son of a bitch, but I think I am in love with the idiot!” I plop down between the two of them.

My mom embraces me in a hug. My dad tries to console me.” We can pay him back.”

I sniff.” No Daddy. I’ll pay him back.”

Mom chimes in, “You really love him?”

“Yes...No.... I don’t know.... he infuriates the hell out of me.”

“That’s love, alright,” Daddy says as he gets up and grabs a tissue.

“What? No. You and Momma aren’t like that.” I take the tissue from him.

“Your daddy used to drive me crazy. One minute I was madly in love with him, the next minute I wanted to chop his balls off.”

“Momma!” I’ve never heard her talk like that.

She shrugs her shoulders at me.” What? It’s true.”

Daddy nods.

“But you two always seem so loving to each other.”

“Sweetie, it takes time and a lot of compromises, but if you love someone it’s worth it. We didn’t just suddenly wake up and have a good strong marriage, we work at it every day.”

I lay my head on her shoulder.” But he and I come from two different worlds. He is super rich. I don’t like that he thinks he can throw money at things and fix it.”

“Well, maybe that is all he knows. You can teach him differently,” Momma says.

“It’s not just that, he has secrets. I can’t get him to talk to me about them.”

Dad’s turn.” You said you love him right?”

I shake my head and tears start falling again.

“I know my daughter well enough, that if you have fallen in love with him, then he is a good man and everything else can be worked out.”

His words make me cry harder.

“Come on now, dry up those tears and let me get you something to eat.” Momma’s answer to problems is always food. And she won’t take no for an answer.

We spend the rest of the day catching up, eating and playing cards. Dad shows me his new project in the barn. He actually seems excited about life now. A big change from the last year, when I worried about his obvious depression. I am thankful to August for lifting his spirits. It's hard to be angry about the money when I see the smile on my dad's face. I still don't know why he lied about work and I have had a little time to think about it. I have to be able to trust him, and I don't. In my mind, all the other issues we have can be worked out, but not trusting him. I need to end it with him before I get in any deeper. He has helped my parents and I'd like to continue working with Tom. Maybe, in turn, it will help August.

The next morning, I lay in bed thinking, until the smell of breakfast wakes my stomach along with my mind. Momma always makes the best breakfast. If I stay here too much longer, I'm going to get fat. I glance over at the clock. Good lord, it's already ten o'clock. I never sleep this late. I jump out of bed and head for the shower.

I throw on a pair of cut-off shorts and one of my favorite old t-shirts I found in the dresser, and my cowboy boots.

As I come down the stairs I yell to Momma about

how good the food smells, but as I round the corner to the kitchen, I stop dead in my tracks. There, sitting at the table, is August. He's dressed in blue jeans and a white button-down shirt. He's is stuffing food in his mouth, and Dad is in deep conversation with him. I guess I should've listened to the fifteen messages he left on my phone.

"Well good morning, sunshine, it's about time you woke up," Momma says.

August stops mid-chew and looks at me. He has food packed in his cheek. My dad breaks the awkward silence. "We have met your friend, August." *Thanks for stating the obvious, Dad.*

August cautiously waves at me. I stomp by him to fix me a cup of coffee and as I pour the creamer, I look down at how I'm dressed. For a moment I'm embarrassed. Then I tell myself, this is the real me if he doesn't like it, then too bad. I turn around and blush when I notice August staring at my ass. My parents seem oblivious, thankfully. I lean against the counter and squint at him as I take a sip of coffee.

Momma seems to finally sense the tension." Um...sweetie.... your dad and I have some work to do upstairs." She grabs dad's plate of food and his hand, dragging him up the stairs as he tries to protest.

I take my cup of coffee and sit at the far end of the table facing August.

"Hi." He says tepidly.

"What are you doing here?"

"You wouldn't answer your phone and I wanted to make sure you were okay."

"When people don't answer their phones, it's because they don't want to speak to you, much less see you."

He starts to stand up." I'd sit back down if I were you," I say. His chair scrapes on the hardwood floor as he sits.

"What did I do that has made you so angry with me?"

"Do you want the list?"

The bastard grins at me. "There's a list?"

"Yes." I see movement on the stairs." We should take this conversation outside." I tilt my head in the direction of the stairs.

We both get up in silence and I direct him into the barn. Beads of sweat are forming on his brow. It's hot here this time of year, and this city boy doesn't know how to dress. I like that he's sweating. It gives me the upper hand. At least that's what my head is saying. My body, however, has a mind of its own and I feel a low burn in my belly.

He steps up close to me and tries to take my hand." Don't touch me," I say. I see the hurt in his eyes and I feel bad. He drops his hand and steps back.

"Can you just tell me what I did wrong?"

He really has no clue." First of all, you paid off my parent's mortgage after I specifically told you not to." My hands are on my hips.

"How I choose to spend my money is none of your business." He has the balls to look angry at me.

"Its my business when it comes to my family and you're solely persuaded when you are fucking me!"

"We're not just fucking!" He yells." And I've told you repeatedly to watch your mouth."

I ignore his rage." If we weren't just fucking, then why do you run off to your private sex club on Fridays instead of working like you told me!?" I'm in his face.

He takes a step back." What the hell are you talking about?"

"I called your office yesterday to tell you some news about Tom, and guess what? You haven't worked on Fridays in years. You leave the house pretending to go to your office and don't come home until Friday night!"

He clinches his jaw again and rakes his hands

through his hair." So you assume I'm out fucking someone?"

"You don't confide in me. What do you want me to think? !"

He takes a deep breath and visually tries to calm himself." I've never had to answer to anyone." His eyes have softened." I'll tell you about my Fridays, but can you just quit yelling at me?" He unbuttons his top two buttons. The heat is starting to get to him. I walk over and turn on a couple of fans. He stands in front of one of them for a few minutes. I grab one of the smaller hay bales and place it in front of the fan and sit down. After a moment, he joins me. He is so quiet.

I place my hand on his." Talk to me, August. Please." All my anger is gone.

"The car accident that dad caused, that killed my mother, hurt someone else very badly." He pauses." Sam was just an infant."

"Sam? The guy you were mountain climbing with when we met?"

"Yes. He had severe spinal damage and was in the hospital for a long time. They didn't think he would live, much less walk again. His mother Claire, was a single parent. His dad left him when he found out Claire was pregnant. She lost everything in that crash."

"You were just a kid yourself."

"Claire sued my dad and the bastard hid all the money so it looked like he had nothing. His lawyers kept him out of jail. I didn't find out until I was in college and I heard him bragging about it. I confronted him and he denied it. So, I did my own digging and found where he hid the money. I told him I found it and that I was going to expose him. That's the night he went out and got drunk and someone hit him while he was parked, and the young man driving was killed. Dad had his stroke after that, and I covered it up to make it look like he died because the family of the man from the second accident came after his money. The money that belonged to Sam and Claire."

He stands up and paces the dirt floor. "I will never forget the day that I met the two of them. I took the money out of my dad's offshore accounts. I invested a chunk back into what is now Rylan Designs. The other half, I took with me and showed up on Claire's doorstep. She was living in a rundown trailer and barely surviving. She was thin as a rail. It took every penny she had to get help for Sam." He swallows hard. I take his hand and pull him back down to sit by me.

"I had to make up for the years of pain my dad caused them. I knew the pain of my mother dying, so I had to help them. I built them a house, which is right down the road from me. I paid off all their medical bills. I hired a therapist for Sam. I paid for Claire to go to college so she could get a good job." He chokes on his words.

"These are all good things, August. Why would you hide it?"

"At first, Claire was skeptical of my intentions. Slowly, she let me in their lives. Claire and Sam have become my family. I spend my entire Friday with them. For years, that's been my happiness. I didn't want anyone to take that away from me. I thought I was going there to make up for what my dad did to them, but I gained so much more. They gave me forgiveness and love."

I get down on my knees in front of him." August, look at me." He does and there are tears in his eyes." You were just a child. None of what happened that night was your fault. I know your dad blamed you and took it out on you, but it wasn't your fault. What you did for them was amazing."

He won't meet my eyes.

"Look at me. I want you to really hear what I'm saying." I touch his cheek and wipe the lone tear that has fallen." I'd never take them away from you. All you had to do was tell me. I need your honesty. You have so many secrets in your life. I don't know how to deal with them. The one thing I do know is that you have to stop seeing yourself as a bad person. You do not have to pay for your father's sins." I laugh to myself." My dad is right. I couldn't love someone who wasn't a good man."

"You love me," he whispers.

"Yes, August. I love you." He draws me into his lap and kisses me deeply.

I.

Love.

You.

Too. He says between kisses. Our tears mingle together. We stop kissing and we hold each other for the longest time. His shirt is drenched in sweat.

"How about we go inside and get you into some different clothes?" I ask.

"Naked. Could we just be naked?"

I laugh. "I always like naked with you, but this is my parent's house. You will not be fucking me here."

He flips me over and my ass is suddenly in the

air. I feel the slap of his hand." I told you to watch your mouth." He says as he rubs the spot.

I should be angry with him, but instead, I find myself completely turned on by that little sting. He pulls me on his lap again, and I delve into his mouth. My wayward hands pull at his shirt until the buttons pop off. I see the storm in his eyes again. He removes my boots one at a time.

"Take those sexy as hell shorts off," he commands.

I quickly do as he asks as he unbuckles his pants. I lick my lips and reach for him." Oh, no you don't." He grabs my wrists." I'll be taking what I want." He pulls me up to him and walks backward to a stall door. He takes my hands and extends them above my head. He wraps a rope around them.

I've never been so turned on in all my life. He stands back and admires me." You are so beautiful." He places one of his hands under my t-shirt and caresses my breast. My nipples are so hard I think they are going to burst. He kisses my other breast, and at the same time, he inserts two fingers inside of me. I gasp.

"You're so damn wet." He speaks into my ear. I pull myself up on the ropes and wrap my legs around his waist, encouraging him inside me. He slaps my ass again and I yelp. He digs his fingers into my bottom as he enters me. His angle is so deep that I come immediately. His thrusts are so powerful, I have one orgasm right after another until he finds his release.

When our breathing finally calms, he reaches up and unties my wrists. He tugs at my hands and rubs my wrists, and he suddenly looks sad.

"I'm sorry. I got carried away." He kisses the redness on my wrists.

"Hey. You didn't hurt me. I loved it." I say as I kiss him." If you were doing something I didn't like, I'd stop you. You've nothing to be sorry for. I have to admit, I thought you spanking me would bother me, but it didn't. This kind of sex is all new to me, but trust me, I'll tell you when to stop."

He smiles." You bring out the animal in me. I can't get enough of you. I want to devour every inch of you all the time. I almost came in my pants like a teenage boy when I saw you in those cutoff shorts and boots."

"Really?" I laugh. "I felt so uncomfortable wearing that in front of you. I thought you would be totally turned off. You with your suits, and button-down shirts."

He pouts." You don't like my suits?"

"You make suits look good. I just love you out of them more." I kiss his cheek quickly with a smacking sound." But, I think we should put some clothes on before my parents come searching for us."

We both scramble for our clothes." You ripped the buttons off my shirt, woman." He shows me.

"Sorry. I got a little carried away, too."

"You can get carried away anytime you want. I'll just have to buy more shirts."

"How about I take you shopping. I recently got paid and I can afford a t-shirt or two." I smile at him.

* * *

We both change clothes. I put on a sundress with my boots and a cowboy hat, but August is dressed in his city slicker clothes.

"God, woman. You are killing me in that dress and hat."

I twirl around for him." You like it?"

"I love what's in it."

"I love you too, August," I grin at him as I say it. It seems so natural.

We head outside, and he opens the limo door for me." We are so not riding in that beast." I laugh. I shut the door and grab his hand. I take him to my dad's beat up, faded red Ford pickup. I open the passenger side door for him.

"You've got to be kidding me."

"Climb in, city boy."

He hesitates but gets inside. I reach around him and buckle him in like he does me." I wouldn't want you to get injured riding on the back roads."

His eyes get big and I laugh at him.

I purposely hit every hole I can on the way into town just to watch him hold on. The town is small, and the only place to buy clothes is at the old general store. I park out front, get out, and wait for August to join me. He doesn't move.

I walk over to his side of the truck and he rolls down the window." Where is the mall?" He asks. He looks terrified.

"This is it. This is our version of the mall."

"I'm not getting out."

I open his door." Come on. I won't let anything bad happen to you."

He reluctantly puts his feet on the ground. I have to drag him into the store like a child.

"Hey, Nash." I hear a familiar voice from behind the cash register.

"Hey, Mrs. Tilley. It's good to see you."

She comes from behind the counter and looks up

and down August with a smile." Who do we have here?"

"This is my friend August."

"Boyfriend." He adds and pulls me close to him.

"He had an um.... shirt accident and I need to buy him a new one."

She laughs." Have fun with that," and walks away.

August gets close to my ear." She looked like she'd eat me alive."

I laugh at him." She's harmless." The clothes are back here. Let's go see what we can find.

I watch him as he looks at the plaid shirts and scrunches his nose. He holds up a pair of wrangler jeans and shows them to me and I laugh out loud at his facial expression. After watching him for endless moments, "Here just let me pick something out for you." I walk over to the t-shirt rack and flip through a couple of them before I see the perfect one for him. It's a faded red color shirt with Ford written across the front. How appropriate. I don't bother showing it to him. I check out with Mrs. Tilley and pull August out of the store before she really does eat him alive.

Once outside, I hand him the bag." Open it."

He pulls it out and starts laughing. To my complete surprise, he takes his button down off and pulls the t-shirt over his head. My heart skips a beat as it stretches over his muscular chest. The band around the arms are also tight, due to his bulging biceps. As I drool over him, I see Mrs. Tilley watching him from the store window. I turn August toward her and point. He smiles at her and waves, then he mutters, "let's get the hell out of here."

He starts for the pickup truck and I grab his hand." I want to take you to my favorite place to eat."

He looks around at the four blocks that make up our rundown downtown." Here?"

"Trust me. They've the best meatloaf and mashed potatoes in town."

"That wouldn't take much." He says under his breath as I tug him across the road.

"You look hot in that t-shirt by the way. I should dress you more often."

"Not on your life sweetheart. Now I know how you felt when I bought you that dress." He slings his arm around my shoulder. For the first time, I really believe that this could really work with him.

I HELP Momma clean up in the kitchen while Daddy and August sit on our old rickety brown flowered couch. Daddy talks about fishing and hunting, and August appears genuinely interested.

"I like him," Momma says, with a gleam in her eye.

I smile at her." Me too, Momma."

"Let's say we finish up here, and challenge the boys to a game of cards."

"Oh, I don't know about August and cards."

"Don't be silly, child. You can tell a lot about a man with a deck of cards in his hand."

"I don't know if August has ever played cards."

I feel his arms wrap around my waist." Bullshit."

"August! Watch your mouth."

"The card game. Sam taught me." He nips at my shoulder and I turn bright red. Momma grins from ear to ear.

* * *

We play cards until midnight. August beats the pants off of us. I will never underestimate him again. Momma and Daddy say their goodnights, and head for bed. I walk August upstairs. "This is your room." I point out the guest room.

He looks confused." I'm sleeping with you."

"On no, you're not. This is my parents' house. You'll sleep in your own room."

He hugs me to his muscular body." You don't think they know I fuck their little girl?" He nips at my nose.

"You know, I should take you over my knee for your potty mouth like you did me."

He kisses my neck." I like the sound of your hand on my ass." He's not making this very easy. I break free of him.

"Go to your room, young man. I'll see you in the morning." I shut my bedroom door. I sort of wish he would follow me, but he doesn't. I change, wash my face, brush my teeth and climb into my twin size bed. Just as well. The two of us would never be able to sleep in this together.

Just as I start to doze off, I feel the weight of my bed shift." August, what are doing?"

"I couldn't sleep in that lonely bed without you."

"This bed is so small. The two of us won't be able to sleep in it."

He kisses my neck." Good. I have no intention of sleeping."

"I've already told you. We are not having sex in my parent's house. The walls are so thin they'll hear us."

He bites my nipple. Argh. The man is insatiable and he's making me the same way.

"Then you better be careful to not make a sound." He strips me bare as he says those words.

I'm so damn easy.

I give into him.

Willingly.

* * *

"ARE you sure you have to leave? You could change your flight and come back with me tonight?" I kiss him as he gets into his limo.

"No, you spend the extra time with your parents. I have paperwork to catch up on. I just wanted to make sure we were okay."

I lean in through the door and kiss him lightly." We're more than okay, and my parents love you."

He grins." What's not to love?"

I watch him as he drives off. I've learned so much about him in a few days. I understand why he thinks his money can fix things. Money made things right with Claire and Sam. I don't think he understands that they would've loved him regardless of his money, just because he cared enough to try and make things right for them. When I think about his childhood, I think that after his mother died, he was never really a child again, so I understand his control issues. I smile as I think of how good he looked in that tight, faded red t-shirt, and I wonder for a moment if I'll ever get him into a pair of boots. The thought makes me a little horny. Until he came along, I never felt like I had a particularly high sex drive. I like that he brought out that side of me.

CHAPTER TWELVE

AUGUST

It took a couple of weeks, but I finally got Nash to agree to move in with me full time. I paid her rent for a year so that Anna wouldn't have to move out. Nash gave me a hard time, but Anna was thrilled.

I took her to meet Claire, and they hit it off right away. Sam flirts with her every chance he gets. If it was anyone else, I'd probably have to kick his ass.

Things are going so good between us. I miss her like hell when I'm at work. I end up texting her during meetings. I would never have thought a woman could distract me from Rylan Designs. Things are hopping with the company, however; we've never had such a good run. I think Nash is my good luck charm, or has good Karma, or both.

In two weeks I have to go overseas for a few days for a business meeting. I asked Nash to go with me, but she insists she's making progress with my father and wants to keep at it. She has refused to tell me what exactly is going on. I check on him every day, and nothing seems different to me. He just stares into empty space. Nash hung pictures on his wall. Photos of my mom, and me as a kid. At first, I was a little irritated about it, but I bit my tongue. I guess that's part of that "relationship compromise" she keeps talking about. I've had to let go of trying to control what she's doing with Dad. After all, that's why I hired her. She's the medical professional, not me.

Since I'm going to be gone for longer than usual, we plan a rock climbing trip in Zion. The Little miss country girl went out and bought us a tent. I have never in my life slept in a tent, and I'm not at all happy about it. How did I lose so much control over the relationship? I smile to myself. I guess I never really had that much control anyway. The only time she submits to me is in bed, and sometimes even that's a struggle. I let her think she wins because everything she does to me feels so damn good. Who am I to deny her such pleasure?

* * *

“Are you ready for our climb?” I yell back at her as I finish strapping on my gear. She has us weighted down with the camping stuff. Everything we could possibly need. I feel like we’re old west pioneers about to cross the mountains, carrying all our belongings on our backs, instead of a couple out for a little bit of fun camping.

She walks by me.” Waiting on you.” She has a bandana wrapped around her hair. It’s so sexy. Now is not the time for a hard on. You can see everything in these climbing shorts. When I reach down to rearrange the boys, Nash starts laughing at me.

“You gotta a problem there?”

“Yea, its name is Nash. Why do you have to look so damn sexy in everything?”

“You prefer I rock climb naked?”

I growl at her and rearrange again.” You’re not helping matters one bit, talking like that.”

She kisses my cheek.” Poor sex starved August.” Then she walks off, laughing.

I've never climbed this area before. It's challenging. We've been able to stay almost side by side for the climb, talking our way through each move. Nash is a strong climber, very calculated. I especially enjoyed the times she climbed in front of me.

We stop about half way up on a ledge to take in the vistas and consume some protein.

"This view is amazing." She says as she drinks from her camel pack.

"This is the best climb ever, and I have the prettiest partner ever." I kiss her.

"We've about another hour to make it to the top. Let's get going."

I let her get several feet above me and I anchor in just above the ledge. I step up and my anchor comes loose. I fall, and my knees bash against the ledge. I catch myself on my safety line.

"August!" she screams. She can't see me below the ledge.

"I'm fine! Keep climbing." I pull myself back up on the ledge. She's sitting there, waiting for me.

"You scared the hell out of me." She's pale.

"I'm okay. I just skinned my knees and my pride."

* * *

The rest of the climb goes smoothly; no more mishaps. We stop again for some water before trekking down to a hidden mountain lake. It's crystal clear and there only a few other people camping. Nash picks a spot right by the water. We're hidden from the other hikers.

I try to help her put up our tent, but I'm pretty useless, so she sends me off to gather some firewood. This place is so pristine that I almost feel like I'm trespassing on mother nature. Chipmunks and rabbits dart in and out of the brush, making little rustling noises. I spook a family of deer, and they take off into the woods with white tails flashing. "Have a nice afternoon, Bambi," I say out loud. I feel so content, and I know it's because of Nash. A cloud covers the sun for a moment, and the woods around me darken. So do my thoughts. It seems too perfect. I keep waiting for something from my past to interfere. I shake off the negative thoughts, and the sun reappears. I smile. *The power of positive thinking.*

The sun goes down, and Nash has the fire going. She's making s'mores.

"I can't believe you've never had s'mores." She says as she builds one for me. She suddenly shakes her head. "I'm sorry. I forget you didn't have much of a childhood. And you did grow up in the city anyway. Maybe not a lot of s'mores and campfires around the skyscrapers." She chuckles sadly.

"Don't be sad for me. I have you to share this with now." I drape my arm around her.

"I love you, August. Thank you for doing this with me. I know you had to warm up to the idea of camping." She laughs.

"What's so funny?"

"The look on your face when I brought home the tent." She laughs again. "Did you expect me to have a butler helicoptered in here?"

"No, but a port-o-potty would be nice." I grab her and tickle her." I'm glad you find me so humorous."

She squeals.

"Shhh. You're going to disturb the other campers." I kiss her lips. She is breathless and beautiful by firelight." If they are going to hear you screaming, I want it to be screams of pure pleasure. Then my name leaving your beautiful pink lips."

"August." She breathes out as she says it.

I stand and take her hand." I want to get thoroughly acquainted with this tent. Or with you in this tent, anyway."

She willingly follows me inside. I slowly divest her of her clothing and mine. I touch every inch of her body and then start over. She begs for me to make love to her. I tell her to hush and continue worshiping her body. When she can stand no more, I roll her on top of me. To my surprise, instead of climbing on me, she scales my body and puts her mouth on my cock. I'm ready to explode, but I don't want to let go yet. She smiles up at me as I inhale, trying to maintain control. Once again, she's flipped the control—in this moment, she owns me. I'm more surprised when I feel the gentle scrape of her teeth against me. I look down at her. She meets my eyes.

"If you think for one second you have control, you better remember my teeth are on your most prized possession." She winks and puts me back in her mouth.

I'm a goner. All I can do is hold on for dear life and let her have her way. Just as I'm about to come, she impales herself on my shaft. She rides me all the way to heaven. I literally see stars.

THE HIKE through the narrows exhilarates us. It's a tough climb, and we both lose our footing more than once. Neither of us cares, however, even when we slip on the banks of a boisterous mountain stream. I don't feel my soaking wet shoes because I'm pretty sure I'm walking on air.

"We need to do this more often," she says as we load up the car.

"I'll camp with you anytime."

"I'm dog tired from your sexcapades last night. I'm looking forward to a good night's sleep." She says as she shuts the car door.

"I'm sorry if I kept you up, but those howling coyotes scared me," I say. teasing her.

"So fear makes you horny?"

"No. But fear kept me awake, and what else was there to do in the middle of the night if you can't sleep?" I shrug my shoulders.

"That's some interesting logic," she says and squeezes my knee.

* * *

THE NEXT TWO weeks pass quickly. On Friday, instead of my usual one on one time with Sam and Claire, the four of us eat pizza and go bowling. Another first for me. To everyone's excitement, Sam manages to walk on his braces the entire night. I'm hopeful that he'll be able to shed even those high-tech crutches soon.

"My new car is so cool," Sam says to me. "You have to let me take you for a drive."

"No thanks," I say. "I bet you speed something awful."

"Did Sam tell you he got accepted into his first choice of colleges?" Claire looks about a foot taller, she's so proud.

"How about that. Good for you." I give him a high five.

"Congratulations," Nash adds.

"Thanks to you, I'll be able to drive myself to the campus, and hopefully, before too long I'll be able to walk the halls, too." He is so excited.

Claire looks a little tearful." I can't thank you enough, August. The day you walked into our lives changed everything for us." She sniffs." The best part is that you became our family." The flood gates let down and she sobs noisily into her hands. The groups of people bowling around us watch with raised eyebrows. Bowling balls grind down the alleys and crash dramatically into the pins, and the place is playing loud country music over the speaker system, so luckily that commotion drowns out most of the noise.

I sit beside Claire and hug her." Thank you for letting me in. Aside from that beautiful blonde sitting across from us, you guys are the best thing that has ever happened to me."

* * *

I CURL up in bed and draw Nash into me." I'm going to miss you this week."

She reaches behind her and places her hand on my cheek." It's only a week." "Yes. But there will be a weekend without you in it. I'll be so busy over there and with the time difference, I'm not sure we'll even get to speak."

"It's okay, August. I'm not going anywhere. I'll be right here when you get back."

"I love you, Nash."

"I love you too, August."

It seems like a simple, easy moment. I have no idea of the chaos, and danger, that's waiting around the corner for us. For me, but especially for Nashville.

CHAPTER THIRTEEN

NASH

I want to get Tom out of the house and get some fresh air. I remove the unused journal from his bed and use the lift to help me get him into the wheelchair I requested from the physical therapist. The therapist thought I was crazy, but he appeased me. When no one else is around, Tom has started speaking a few words. He says my name, clearly. He tries to smile when I talk to him about August. I swear he chuckled when I told him I took August camping, and that he was scared of the coyotes. Of course, I didn't tell him what August did to conquer his fear. That's not exactly the kind of conversation one has with her lover's father, even if he can't talk back to me.

"All set. Are you ready to go outside?"

He nods.

This is the first time I have used the elevator. The hired help comes in through this way. August doesn't like people walking through the house. Stella and I are allowed, of course, but no one else.

I wheel Tom down to the lake. I brought a blanket, so I can sit, and some bread so we can feed the ducks. If no one is watching, maybe Tom will enjoy feeding them himself.

I place some crumbs in his hand. "It's okay. It's just you and me."

He peers around him before making a weak toss. These ducks are practically tame, and they come waddling and quacking toward us, poking each other with their bills, fighting over the best chunks of bread. I am glad he is so responsive to me, but it saddens me that he won't react to August.

"Why me? Why do you only let me in, and no one else?" I ask him.

He whispers, "Augie."

"Is it because I love August?"

He nods.

"Don't you love August?" It makes my heart hurt that I even have to ask him.

He closes his eyes tight as if he in pain, but he doesn't say anything. He still betrays how he feels, however, with a single tear that rolls down his weathered face. Tom does love his son.

"Why won't you let him see you?"

He chokes out a single word." Sara."

"You can't still blame August for her death," I say, feeling defensive. Tom's tears flow freely now, so maybe he's trying to tell me something else. I stand and hold his face between my hands. He opens his eyes.

"August is a good man. He will forgive you if you let him."

There's a rustling sound behind me, from the other side of the wall that surrounds the property. For some reason, it doesn't sound like a rabbit or even a coyote. I get the creeping feeling I'm being watched. Tom's eyes dart back and forth. I stand and look around. I don't see anything, but the feeling still remains. And what could have been big enough to make that noise? A mountain lion, maybe, but they usually hide away in the hills. And besides, it just sounded like human feet running. I pack up my blanket and keep a watchful eye out as I push Tom back to the house.

When I get him settled back in his room, I call the guard at the gate. He says he has not seen anyone on the security cameras. I can't shake the feeling that

I was being watched. I try August's cell phone, but it's the middle of the night overseas. I get his voicemail.

"Hey, August. I miss you." I don't want to worry him for something that was

just a weird feeling and a strange noise. "Nothing happening here. Just wanted to hear your voice."

I lay down, and fall into a restless sleep. I'm jolted awake by my phone ringing in the middle of the night.

"Hello." My eyes have not focused enough to see the number on the phone.

"Hey, baby. I'm sorry I missed your call earlier today."

I sit up and clear my throat." It's okay, I just missed you."

"I know it's the middle of the night for you, but I wanted to make sure you were okay."

"I'm fine. I just missing being in your arms. How is work going?"

"We've had a few glitches here and there, but nothing I can't handle."

"I wish you were home handling me right about now."

"Me too. You've no idea how much."

I yawn into the phone.

"Go back to sleep and dream of me," he says. "I'll send you my flight schedule by the end of the week. I love you, Nash."

"I love you, too," I say. This time, I sleep more soundly, comforted by the sound of his voice.

I DON'T TAKE Tom outside the rest of the week. That strange encounter, or non-encounter, or whatever it was, has me spooked. I entertain myself by playing cards with Tom. It's slow and monotonous, but he can manage to say "go fish," and he can hold his own cards. Anna is coming over to hang out tonight. I have to be careful to not mention Tom and limit her tour of the house to downstairs. She doesn't know that I'm still working for August. She assumed that stopped when I moved in with him full time.

I give Stella the night off and order Chinese food. Anna picks it up on her way over.

She almost drops the brown paper bag of kung pao chicken and sauce packets. "Oh my god, Nash, this house is fabulous." She walks in a circle, staring at the vaulted ceilings and admiring the art on the walls." What's upstairs? I bet he has an attic with hidden treasures. I want to see your bedroom! Is it huge?" She walks toward the stairway.

"Wait. I have something even better to show you." I want to distract her, so I lead her through the house to the infinity pool.

"It just keeps getting better. No wonder you moved in here." She starts peeling off her clothes.

"Anna, what are you doing?" I say, laughing.

"What does it look like? Skinny dipping." The splash of the cold water hits my face as she dives in. "Aren't you coming in?" she asks when she comes up for air.

"My girlfriends and I use to sneak in the river at home and skinny dip. I haven't done this in forever." I say as I strip out of my clothes. We swim and laugh for the next hour. As we are getting out I hear a noise in the cabana. I go cold. It reminds me of what happened the other day when I had Tom outside in his chair. A rustling, and maybe running feet.

"Did you hear that?" I whisper to Anna.

"Yea, but it is so dark. I don't see anything." She whispers back. I reach for some towels out of a cabinet." Do you think we should check it out?"

She wraps her towel around her." It's probably just an animal."

"I don't know. I've the eeriest feeling that someone has been watching me the last few days."

"I'm sure you are just being paranoid in this big house with August gone."

"Maybe." We walk into the house, and I say, "I'm going to flick on all the lights outside. You keep watch, and tell me if you see anything."

"Okay." She stands at the glass doors.

I flip the lights on, and then off.

"Nothing," she says. "I'm sure it was just some kind of critter. Let's eat. I'm starving."

Anna has a one track mind, but I'm still not satisfied that the visitor was just a critter. Twice in a few days is too much of a coincidence.

* * *

We eat like pigs and stay up until two in the morning watching movies. We sleep on the enormous leather couch. I brought down pillows from August's bed, and we wrapped up in soft cashmere blankets. Mine is green, and Anna's is red. She jokes that we look like Christmas decorations.

I wake up to the smell of coffee. Anna is still asleep, with her arm dangling off the couch. I get up and join Stella in the kitchen.

At nine, I wake Anna and scoot her out the door so that I can work with Tom. I've decided that I'm going to update August on his father's progress. It's about time—there's no point in keeping it from him anymore. Now that I know Tom loves August, it will be easier to tell him. I just hope Tom cooperates with my plan. Who knows, he might just lay there, staring into space. Then I'll look like a crazy person.

I take a late night swim, and I make sure to turn on all the lights before I jump into the pool. It tires me out, which is exactly what I want. I'm afraid I won't be able to sleep. August will be home tomorrow, and I'm so excited. I can't wait to see him. I toss and turn for a while, but finally, I drift off.

A shuffling noise jolts me awake. I was dreaming about something—I can hardly remember—but maybe it was a mountain lion. My eyes haven't adjusted to the dark, but I see a shadow pass the doorway. I know I closed the door behind me.

"Who's there?" I call out. I hear the elevator doors shutting. I grab my robe and tiptoed down the hall. I never thought to ask August if he keeps a gun in the house. If I had one, I'd feel safer, even if I can't imagine ever actually using it on someone. *Let's hope it's not coming to that kind of thing,* I think. My mind doesn't want to be convinced this time. Unless a mountain lion climbed down the chimney, it seems unlikely an animal is making noise and casting flitting shadows on the wall. I walk into the living room, and nothing is disturbed. I check on Tom—he's asleep. The aide sits beside him with headphones on. My fears deflate some. Maybe it was just the remnants of a bad dream. All appears peaceful now.

Still, I struggle to fall asleep again. I can't wait for August to come home. I stare into the darkness, looking for movement until my body begins fighting my mind. My eyelids get heavy. The last time I remember looking at the clock it was four thirty in the morning.

I wake up to someone touching the small of my back. I flip over and almost scream.

"Oh my god August, you scared the shit out of me!" I clutch my chest.

He holds up his hands. "Whoa! Sorry. You're jumpy." He sits on the bed with me.

I shake my head, trying to clear the dusty residue of an unpleasant and restless night. "You're early. You should have called me." I kiss his cheek.

"Baby, it's noon," he says and laughs.

I crawl into his lap and snuggled against his neck." Wow! Really. I didn't sleep well last night."

"I didn't sleep either. I was thinking about

coming home to you, and all the things I want to do to you." He rubs my thigh.

"I kept hearing noises. All night. I could have sworn someone was in the house." I say into his neck.

He leans back and looks into my face." Why didn't you call me?"

"Because I decided it was only my imagination. I had a bad dream. I'm sure it was just nerves and you being gone and—"

He's already standing up, and talking into his phone." Wayne, I want you to review the security tapes from my house last night." He hangs up." Did anything seem out of place?"

"No. Nothing. The other night when Anna came over, we both heard something in the cabana as we were getting out of the pool, but we didn't see anything. We assumed it was an animal." He still looks worried, which bothers me." Is there something I should know? Are you in some kind of danger?"

He holds me to him." No. No, of course not. I'm sure it was nothing. I have security cameras all over this place. If there was someone here, Wayne will notify me." He kisses the top of my head.

"Good, now can we go back to bed?" I bat my eyes.

"I need a shower. How about you take this less

than adorable Hello Kitty shirt off and join me." He pulls me with him toward the shower.

"You have something against Hello Kitty?" I tease him.

"No, but I have something against anything that prevents me from seeing your beautiful body right now." He lifts my arms over my head and slips off my shirt." That's more like it." He stands back and admires me.

"My turn." I pull at his hem, remove his shirt, and then unbuckle his pants. When I pull him free, he's already hard." You're ready for me." That's what he usually says to me.

"I've been ready for you since I boarded the plane. I don't think I'm going to last very long." He pulls me into the shower with him. I reach down to stroke him, but he pulls my hands away. He turns me around, so my back is to him, and gently pins my hands to the shower wall." There is not a chance in hell I'm going to let you touch me until I've had my hands on you." His voice in my ear and the water hitting the center of my back make me shiver. He spreads my legs and inserts a finger." You're already so damn wet for me, baby." He takes my wetness and traces it to my backside. I'm startled when he slowly inserts a finger." I want to have you here." He bends and kisses the middle of my back.

"I don't think so,"I say as he inserts another finger.

He pinches my nipple with his other hand and traces his tongue along the outside of my ear." That wasn't a no. Is that your final answer?"

What he is doing feels so damn good." I...I...don't know." I barely get the words out before he releases my nipple and finds my clit. He pinches and pulls, and his fingers continue there, in and out of my rear.

"I'm only going to ask you one more time baby? Is that a no?"

"No. I mean not a no."

He bends me over and teases me with the tip of his cock. He slowly pushes inside. At first, there is a burning pain, but as he goes deeper, the pain turns to pleasure. It's a fullness I've never experienced. When I gasp, he goes still.

"Are you okay?" He sounds as if he's on the edge of control. He reaches around and rubs my clit.

"Yes. Oh, god, yes."

He pulls part way out and thrust in harder this time. He grabs my hips. His fingers are going to leave a mark, and I could not care less. I push back against him, and he groans.

“Be still,” he says.

He’s getting harder inside me, and it makes me lose control. My body convulses in an orgasm. He pants as my body tightens around him.

“You. Feel. So. Fucking. Good.” He says between each punishing thrust. As another orgasm spirals through me, he releases his own energy in a rush, calling my name.

He pulls out of me and spins me around. He kisses me like a starving man who has just been presented with a gourmet meal.

“I think you missed me,” I say as I hold his cock in my hands. It’s still hard.

“I’m nowhere near done with you.” He picks me up and thrusts into me again and again and again, until we are both limp, like two overcooked noodles. My legs are barely holding me up, and his thighs are visibly trembling. We gingerly step out of the shower, dry each other off, and lay naked in each other’s arms until we fall asleep.

I wake just as it’s getting dark, and look at the clock. Late evening. August is deeply asleep, his chest lightly rising and falling. Maybe it’s jet lag. *Or maybe it’s so much amazing sex,* I think, and suppress a giggle. I gently untangle from him and climb out of bed. There’s some pain in my bottom, where he intruded me in the shower. The pain doesn't bother me, but the memory makes me shiver. I could never have imagined someone could make me comfortable with those kinds of sexual escapades, yet here I am, comfortable as a cat on a warm window ledge. I watch him sleeping for a moment, my heart swelling with love, before grabbing my robe and walking downstairs. I'm painfully hungry. I didn't eat much yesterday, and so the combination of too few calories and too much exertion is kicking in hard. Stella is just cleaning up as I enter the kitchen.

"Hey," I say.

She smiles at me." You two never came down for dinner."

I blush. There's really nothing I can say to that. Of course, she knows what we were doing." Is there anything left over from dinner?"

She pulls out two containers and warms them up. I pick a bottle of wine and ask her if she'd like to join me. She agrees, so we sit beside one another at the bar. I have a plate and a glass. She just has a glass." Are you hungry?" I ask. I realize I never see Stella eat.

"I eat so much as I cook, I'm rarely hungry." She shrugs.

"That makes sense. This is nice. You and I never

get to eat together. Or me eating and drinking and you just drinking." I wink at her, but she doesn't laugh. I find that odd. She's always jolly. "Is there something wrong?" I ask.

"I like you, Nash," she says. "You're very good for Mr. Rylan."

"August is very good for me too." I smile and blush again.

"I worry about your work with his father. Tom was not good to Mr. Rylan. Even talking about that situation brings out the worst in him. Young Mr. Rylan has had to lie, just to cover up for his father, too many times. I don't want you to hurt him by dredging up the past."

I take her hand in mine." That's the last thing I want to do. I think I can actually help them. Both of them."

"Just be careful dear." She hugs me to her. "You know, it's not surprising to me that Mr. Rylan would end up with a nurse."

"Why?" I say. "Oh, because of his scholarships? I know he said the nurses were kind to him as a child in the hospital after the accident."

She nods. "It was more than kindness to that boy. I think it was probably the last time he felt as if it was okay to grieve. There, with those women who took care of him while he was hurting. Inside, and out."

I touch Stella's knee. "That's what I want to do for him, too. Take care of him, inside and out."

* * *

I DON'T FEEL TIRED, so I decide to explore the wall of books in August's office for something to read. Most of them are business related, but there are a few on mountain climbing, geography, and history. I skim my hand across the titles as I move further down the wall. One book stands out for its sheer basicness— a small brown volume with gold lettering. *Little Women* by Louisa May Alcott. I turn the worn pages. In the front is a handwritten quote from the book.

"Someday you'll find a man, a good man, and you'll love him, and marry him, and live and die for him."

I trace the words. The handwriting is feminine. Sara must have written it. How beautiful. I assume she wrote it about Tom— she must've really loved him. I think about how different all of their lives could've been had the accident never happened. August would've had two loving parents. He himself would be so different. Would he love me? Would I love him? Our worlds would probably never have collided. Sam and Claire's life would have been different. My eyes well up as I picture that eight-year-old boy losing his mother, and grieving alone in the hospital with gentle nurses holding his hand, and his world further falling apart as his father spiraled out of control. I feel a little guilty that I have August in my life. It's really because of this tragedy that we found one another.

I think about the quote Sara wrote. I've found a "*good man.*" I "*love him.*" I would *"live and die for him."* I can't bring his mother back, or change his past, but I can damn sure try to make things better in his future. I believe I can even return some of his lost father. Maybe Tom and August could be close again.

I settle onto the leather sofa and flip through a few more pages. A picture falls out—Tom and Sara's wedding picture. They look so happy and in love. On the back, there's a note.

"My dearest August, I want you to have a love like this. I love you. Mom"

I wonder if August has ever even seen this picture. I place the photo and the book on the glass coffee table. I approach the piano, Sara's piano, and touch the keys. I haven't played much over the past few years. It's not exactly easy to fit a piano in a little apartment. I took years of lessons, however, and used to play at my church when I still lived in Tennessee. I love the thought that his mother used to sit down at this very piano and play for August. When I sit down, it all comes back to me. I softly play a few pieces I've memorized.

"WHAT THE FUCK do you think you're doing?"

The angry voice behind me makes me jump, and I bang out a few jarring notes. My knees hit the piano, and the wooden cover of the keyboard slams down on the keys. I'm lucky I don't lose a finger. August is shirtless, breathing hard, and his jaw is jutting at me like an accusatory finger.

"I'm sorry. I didn't mean to wake you up." I walk toward him, intent on hugging him, but he holds me away from him. It's so hurtful and surprising, I feel like he slapped me. I've never seen him angry, and it makes no sense to me." Why are you mad?"

"Who told you that you could touch her piano?"

"I didn't realize I needed permission."

"Some things in this house are not yours to touch."

Suddenly, I'm pissed." Oh really? I thought I

lived here, too. Am I supposed to consult a check sheet before touching anything?"

He runs his hands through his hair. "You're right. This is our house." He's still shaking, but at least he's not yelling.

"When you talk to me like that, it sure doesn't feel like our house." I try to see it from his perspective. I know how touchy he is about his mother." But I'm sorry I upset you. I wouldn't have touched it had I known."

He walks toward me, and I think he's going to take me in his arms, but then he notices the book and the picture on the coffee table. His nostrils flare." The piano isn't the only thing you've been messing around with. Why were you in my office, anyway? Snooping through my things?"

That stings. "I couldn't sleep. I thought I could find something to read."

He slams the book on the table." You have no right to be in my mother's things!"

I try to rationalize with him. Maybe this is a bit of that traumatized eight-year-old boy showing up again. "August, have you seen that picture?" I pick it up and try to hand it to him, but he won't take it." Look at it. They were happy. He made her happy." I turn it over and show him her note to him.

He takes it from me. A chuffing sound escapes his throat, and tears run down his face." She deserved better than him."

I touch his tears." He made her happy. He lost her, too. You know that's what changed him. Neither of you could get over your grief. He shriveled up inside."

He steps away." I don't give a fuck what it did to him!He killed her! Then he made me miserable! Look what he did to Sam. Without remorse. Don't defend him to me!"

"I'm not defending him. I'm defending her." I'm getting frustrated. "If your mother loved him, he had to be a good man at one point. I'm sorry that he hurt you, but he's still here, and you take care of him for a reason. There must be a part of you that loves him or is willing to forgive him. If you hated him that much, you'd have sent him to a nursing home."

"I have other reasons for keeping him here."

That makes no sense to me. "Like what? Why else would you go to all this effort?"

"I don't want to talk about it."

"But—"

"I think we've both said enough for tonight." He turns and stalks out.

Once he disappears, I grab my purse and rush to

my car. I cry as I jam the key into the ignition. The old Mustang roars to life, and it's dependable. Predictable. Understandable. I want to scream. August will never let me in. He either can't, or he won't. I step on the gas and drive toward the front gate. The guard is talking to someone on the phone, but when I beep he opens the gate. I dial up Anna to make sure she is home. She's my safe place, and I need someone and something familiar right now. Not August and his erratic, unexplainable behavior. She can hear the tears in my voice.

"I don't know what happened," she says, "but you make sure you drive safely."

I'm not so far gone that I don't notice the person tail gaiting me. At first, it's just annoying, but as the lights from that car blast into mine mile after mile, I realize something terrifying. As I approach the apartment complex, I wait until the last second to turn. The guy behind me almost runs into me, but he can't make the turn. He keeps going past the complex. I part and run up to my old apartment, my heart beating in my chest.

"Someone was following me," I say, as I look back over my shoulder and slip inside.

"What? I'm calling the police." Anna slides the deadbolt and reaches for her phone.

"No, let me call August first." I step into my old bedroom and call him, but it goes straight to voicemail. I send him a text rather than leave a voicemail. It's faster.

I know you're mad at me, but I'm starting to get really scared. Someone was following me tonight. Please call me.

"What the hell is going on?" Anna asked.

"I don't know. August and I got in a fight, and—" My throat is blocked by a huge lump of mixed emotions. She sits on the couch and pats the space beside her. Like I have so many times over the years, I sit next to her and tell her everything. Well, everything I can tell her, anyway.

We talk about the book, the picture, me playing the piano, and August freaking out on me.

Her brows come together, and Anna looks decidedly put off my August's behavior. "I don't want you going back there. I'm starting to think he's either nuts or involved in some really fishy stuff. Or maybe both."

"I'd agree with you if I didn't love him," I say between sobs.

"I know you love him, but he needs to get his shit together." She hands me a tissue.

My phone lights up with August's face and

before I can answer it Anna grabs it from me. I can hear August on the other end asking to speak to me, but Anna refuses. She tells him to call the police and to leave me the hell alone. She hangs up the phone and even turns in off. I cry even harder.

CHAPTER FOURTEEN

AUGUST

It has been two weeks since my fight with Nash. I keep trying her phone, but she won't answer. I even went to her apartment, but Anna gave me an earful and insisted that Nash wasn't there. Turns out she was telling the truth. It didn't take long to track down her plans. She went to Tennessee to see her parents. I'm packing, just throwing a few things in a bag, ready to go after her, when Wayne calls.

He's all business, as usual. "That night Nash and Anna went swimming? Outside cameras got an unclear glimpse of someone leaving the cabana. The cameras inside the house were down."

"What do you mean they were *down?*"

"They appear to have malfunctioned, sir."

"Why am I just now fucking learning of this?"

"I wasn't informed either. I'm looking into it."

"You do that, Wayne. That's what I pay you for." I hang up, sit on the bed, and rub my eyes.

For her safety, I know I can't follow her. My stomach clenches with remorse. I was such as ass to her that last night. I was so angry when I heard the piano? No one has touched it since my mother died. Mom used to give me lessons, but I quit playing when I lost her. It didn't seem right then, and it still doesn't seem right now. Still, I took my anger out on the one person who didn't deserve it. I've been a mess since she left. If I'm not going to find her, I decide to go see Sam. He keeps bugging me to come over. Says he has to show me something.

I'm so distracted by my racing thoughts that I feel like I step in the car one second, and into Claire's house the next.

"You look like hell," Claire says as she closes the door behind me.

"Thanks. I feel like hell." I've never been able to lie to her.

"When is the last time you ate?" She leads me into the kitchen.

"I honestly don't remember. Stella has had the flu, and I haven't really been too interested in cooking." I sit down at the table.

"Okay. So then I'm feeding you. You can tell me what happened while you eat."

I catch her up between bites of food.

"So that's it? You're just going to let her go without a fight?" The look on her face is both incredulous and angry.

"What am I supposed to do? My life has been so screwed up for so long. That's not going to change."

"I think it's more like you're not willing to change your life." She leans against the counter and crosses her arms.

"I can't change the things that my father has done."

"Of course, you can't. But you can make decisions that change the outcome of your life, and other people's lives. Sam and I would still be living in that rundown trailer if you hadn't come for us. You changed all of that for us, but you're not willing to go to any effort for the woman you love?" She turns away to wash dishes. Her disappointment washes over me as if she dumped the dirty dishes on my head.

I think about that photo of my parents that Nash showed me, and I imagine my mother would say the same thing. "I don't know what to do," I say. "I know that since she walked out, I've been pathetic. I could never imagine another person could have this much of an effect on me."

"That's called love, August." Claire squeezes my shoulder.

"What did I miss?" I hear behind me.

"Nothing." I turn around, and for a moment, my troubles are forgotten at the sight of Sam, standing, with no additional support. "Sam, where are your braces?"

"That's what I wanted to show you." He slowly walks toward me." I've been walking without them for a week now. I'm a little slow, but the therapist says that will get better with time." He is all smiles. "I wanted to show you in person, not tell you over the phone. Where's Nash? I want to show her, too" he looks around the room.

"She went home to visit her parents for a few days."

Claire leans into me." See? There are things that you can fix, even when they're not your fault. Look at my son, there walking. I think you have some crow to eat." She pats me on the shoulder.

"When are we going climbing again? This time, I won't even need my braces."

"Whoa. Not so fast, Speed Racer." Claire laughs at his enthusiasm.

"I promise we'll go hiking soon. And Nash will come with us." I smile at him, but I'm not at all sure I'll be able to win her back. The thought makes my stomach feel hollow as if the very center of me has been carved out.

I DECIDE I can't wait for her to come back, shadowy figure in the security video or not. I have to go after her. My flight to Tennessee is rocky. A storm grounds most of the commercial flights, but I tell my pilot we're going, storm or no storm. When we finally land, I rent a Ford Pickup truck instead of my usual limo. Maybe it will make me more endearing to Nash. *You're desperate,* I think. And then I agree with myself. *You're right. I am desperate.*

It's pouring rain when I pull up to her parents' farm. I'm not sure what to expect. She has no idea I'm coming. *What if she refuses me?* My heart slams in my ears as I sit in the pickup truck, watching the rain run down the windows in little rivets. Finally, I decide that the agony of awaiting her reaction is worse than whatever it may be. If she's going to break my heart, I might as well get it over with. I open the door and sprint toward the house.

I knock, a dripping, sopping mess, and wait for my fate. Her father George answers the door. He looks none too happy to see me.

"Mr. Jacoby." I stick out my hand. He doesn't offer his. People usually don't make me nervous, but his glare is throwing me off." I'm here to see Nashville."

"I don't think that's such a good idea, son."

"I know she's angry with me and things between us got a little out of hand, but..." It seems weird to be saying this to her father, but it's the truth. "I love her."

He sighs. But he opens the door wider for me to come inside.

"Wait just a minute. Nancy! Bring me a towel," he calls over his shoulder." You drip all over Nancy's rugs, you'll have more than one angry woman to deal with."

Nancy comes into the foyer with a periwinkle blue towel tucked under her arm. "Did you track mud on my rugs? I told you to take off your shoes with this rain—" She stops when she sees me, half in and half out of the door. "Oh...August...I didn't know you were coming."

"Just hand the boy the towel," George says.

She holds it at arms length as if she'd be betraying her daughter by getting too close to me. "Nash isn't here right now. She went out for some groceries and got stuck in the storm. She's going to wait around town before coming home. The water rises around the little bridge over Cross Creek in these kinds of storms."

"At this rate, it might stay that way until tomorrow," George says.

"Is she at the General store?" I ask.

"Yes," her mother says.

I turn to leave. George grabs my arm. "You can't go back out in this."

"I didn't come this far to wait one minute longer to make things right with her."

Her father lets go of my arm. If anything, I feel him gently push me out the door.

THE FRONT DOOR chimes as I enter the general store. No one is at the front counter, but I hear laughter coming from a back room.

"Hello," I call out.

"Can I help you?"

It's the same lady that was here before. I can't recall her name. She has that same look on her face as before. Like she'll eat me for breakfast along with her biscuits and gravy.

"I'm looking for Nash." As I say her name she walks into the room. She stares at me in shock.

"What are you doing here?" She crosses her arms.

"Is there someplace we can speak privately?" I glance between her and the scary store owner.

Nash takes my hand and leads me to the front door. I assume she's going to shove me out the door, but she says, "Let's sit in your limo to talk." She grabs a big black umbrella on the way out. It opens with a swish and almost pokes out my eye.

"Where's your car?"

I feel like I can win some points, so I press the button on my keychain and the pickup truck's lights flash. As I open the truck door, she stares at me." This is what you drove?" I can tell she's trying to not smile.

"Would you just get in before we are swept away?"

She squints at me." Say please."

I want to throw her over my knee and spank her for being so defiant, but that's probably not the best way to win her back. "Please. Will you get in the truck?"

To my surprise, she climbs into the truck. I close the umbrella and throw it in the truck bed. When I get in, she's leaning against the passenger door. She looks ready for battle.

"Why are you here?" she asks.

For a moment, all I can do is stare at her, she's that beautiful. I wonder if she's been as miserable as I've been. God, I have missed her.

"Did you come all this way just to gawk at me?" she asks. "Or do actually have something you want to say?"

"I was an idiot."

"Go on."

"I behaved very poorly. I'm very sorry."

"And?"

I should have known she wasn't going to let me off easy." I've been desolate since you left."

"Desolate." She snorts." Try another word."

"It means...."

"I know what the fuck it means. I want you to say something more human!"

I grit my teeth." Heartbroken." She's not giving

me an inch, so I refuse to give her a centimeter." Watch your mouth."

To my surprise, she burst out laughing." What's so funny?"

"You. You come here to apologize, yet you still want to control me. Telling me what to say? Please. Whatever comes out of my mouth, it's my choice."

I move closer to her." You know how to do better things than say nasty words. I know what that mouth can do. And it's not always about what comes out of it. What about what goes in it?"

She leans in closer." I don't think you want my mouth on any part of your body right now." She tries to open the door. I grab her from behind and pull her toward me.

"I'm sorry, Nash. I love you." When I whisper, she stops moving.

"I need you," I continue. "My life is worth nothing without you. I was a total asshole. But I recognize it. I'll try to change. For you, I'll do anything."

She relaxes into me and I loosen my grip. She turns in my arms." I still want to know why?"

I know exactly what she is talking about. Why do I take such good care of my father? I suppose I finally have to talk about it. "I remember how he looked at my mother. How much he loved me. I felt guilty for being so childish the night of the accident. If they'd not had to pick me up, she would be alive. He wouldn't have become my enemy. The hate in his eyes for me was more than I could bear. I could handle his beatings, but I could never handle the hate on his face for me."

"Oh my god August, he beat you?" Her hand is on my thigh.

"Don't feel sorry for me. I deserved it."

"No child deserves to be beat. You were in just as much pain as he was. He should've gotten help for both of you."

I let go of her and drape my arms over the steering wheel." The last fight we had, before his stroke, I told him I hated him. He was trying to tell me he was sorry. I think he finally got it. But I wasn't ready to hear it. So he told me he was sorry, and I told him I hated him. That is the last conversation I had with my father."

"He knows you didn't mean it. He loves you."

I chuckle." He doesn't have the ability to feed himself, or think. He doesn't know how to love some-one. I know he had that capacity once, but it's gone now."

She squeezes my knee. "That's not true. You

know I've been working with him. He responds to me. I meant to tell you the day I left." She takes my face in her hands." I can prove it to you when we get back."

"That means you forgive me for the way I treated you?" I plead with her blue eyes.

"I forgive you because you let me in. That's all I ever wanted from you." She lightly kisses my lips.

The lightning cracks and she jumps. When she flinches in my arms, I seize the moment. I kiss her the way I've been wanting to kiss her for the past few weeks." I am so sorry." I keep repeating it between kisses. She slips her hands under my shirt. I unbutton her top and unhook her bra. Her nipples are pert and pink. She moans as I gently suck on them.

"I've missed your mouth," she says. I lean her back on the seat of the truck. Wind and rain pound on the truck. The windows steamed up from our collective heat. It reminded me of that scene in the movie *Titanic* when Rose and Jack make love in the old Model-T and leave the misty handprint on the window. I've never thought about a romantic movie scene outside of watching it in my life. Nashville has done crazy things to my mind, as well as my body.

"I can't wait a minute longer to be inside you." I

tug at her shorts and rip off her delicate panties. I sit up and pull myself free of my jeans. I pull her on top of me, so I'll be able to see her. She braces herself, one hand on the back of the seat, one hand on the ceiling. I tease her with the head of my cock and look up at her. She bites her lip and slowly lowers herself onto me. My whole length is inside her, filling her to the brim.

I grab her hips. "You're so damn tight. If you keep moving like that, I'll lose it." I say between clenched teeth.

She puts her hands on my shoulders. "I want you to lose control with me. Let me do the work this time." She slides up and down, teasing me— slowly up, the down hard, taking me all in. I come, and with so much upward force, her head hits the roof. It doesn't bother her. She keeps riding me until she comes herself. She collapses against me.

"Is your head okay?" I ask, as I stroke her hair. "I didn't mean to hurt you."

"I'm fine. I love you."

"Oh, I forgot." I reach for the glove box.

"You forgot that I loved you?"

"I guess I did for a few weeks, but that's not what I meant." I hand her a silver velvet box.

"What's this?" She takes it.

"It's to remind you that you have my heart even when I am acting like an asshole."

She laughs. "This box isn't big enough."

"I've even missed your smart mouth. Open it."

She holds up a delicate silver bracelet. A diamond heart dangles from it, catching sunlight as it drifts through the dissipating clouds." It's beautiful. But you know you don't have to buy me gifts, right?"

"I wanted you to have it. You're my heart. I know I don't have to buy you anything, but this means something to me. Please don't return it."

She smiles down at me." I'll cherish your heart, August. This one—" She holds up the bracelet. "—and this one." She touches my chest.

* * *

As THE RAIN LETS UP, we drive back to her parents' house. She rubs my thigh. "This truck is a good look on you."

"Don't get used to it. This is temporary. I just did it to impress you."

She pouts at me." We can't do what we just did in the Jaguar. It's way too small.

"Baby, if there's a will there is a way. I can figure

out a way to fuck you in that car. We're both flexible and the seats recline."

She laughs. "Game on. You better work on your yoga poses. My dad is really pissed at you, you know."

"I know he was, but I think I made up for it by informing him of just how much I love you."

"Honestly, I think he enjoys having you around. Usually, it's just him and me and my mom. He's outnumbered."

It's a good chance to tell her what's on my mind. Or at least as much as I can tell her. "He's going to enjoy your company for a little while longer. But not mine."

"What? I'm going back with you."

"I'd prefer you stay here a while longer."

"Why?"

"It's not safe at my house. Turns out you were right. There was someone in the cabana the night you and Anna went for a swim. I know this is scary, but I think someone has probably been in the house. And let's not forget you being followed. The cameras have been malfunctioning all over the property."

"Sounds like an inside job to me. Have you interviewed the staff?"

"Smart girl. Wayne is working on it."

"I'm still going back with you. I'm not going to let anyone scare me off."

"Nash—"

"August." She says, and she doesn't have to say anything else. I'm not arguing with her.

CHAPTER FIFTEEN

AUGUST

"It's so good to be home." Nash kisses me on the cheek as we walk in the door. I stop her and take both her hands.

"I want you to be vigilant. Report anything out of the ordinary. Do you promise me?"

"I promise. After we change and grab a bite to eat, can we go see Tom?"

"Okay, but I don't want you to get your hopes up."

We find Stella in the kitchen. I told her we were coming, and she promised to make up something special.

Nash hugs her. "Are you feeling better? I heard you had the flu."

"I'm much better now. Mr. Rylan sent his doctor to see me, and he fixed me right up. It's so good to have you back." Stella beams at Nash.

"I'm starving," I say. "What's for dinner?"

Stella laughs." I'm glad to see your appetite is back."

"You do look like you've lost weight." Nash frowns at me.

"Think about it. You left me. Stella has been sick. So I've had no appetite and no decent food to tempt me." I swat her playfully on the ass, and she yelps. Stella laughs again. I can tell she's genuinely thrilled to have Nashville home again. Nash makes the whole house feel warmer and more alive.

"Sit down and let me feed you both." She's made fish and roasted potatoes in some kind of light lemon sauce. I couldn't order anything better in a five-star restaurant.

When we finish, Nash rubs her eyes. "It's getting late. Your father can wait until tomorrow. He's better in the mornings. Besides, I have a surprise for you."

"I'm not crazy about surprises."

"If you meet me upstairs in our room in ten minutes, I promise you'll love surprises." She whispers and kisses my ear. Stella regally ignored us as she washes dishes and wipes down the countertops.

"You have eight minutes," I say.

She winks and whispers back, "Then I'd better hurry."

I WASN'T KIDDING when I said that I don't like surprises. I look at my watch, but it's only been two minutes. Stella is talking to me about something, but all I hear is background noise and the anxious thoughts humming between my own ears. What the hell is she up to?

Another two minutes have passed, and I decide I'm done waiting. I take the stairs two at a time. I open the bedroom door, and Nash is standing at the end of the bed with her cowboy boots on.

Only her cowboy boots. God, I love this woman.

I shut the door behind me. "Well, this is a *nice* surprise."

She has her hands behind her back. She's hiding something. "Watcha got there, pretty lady?" I ask, smiling.

She grins at me and reveals a long rope. She holds it out toward me.

"A lasso?" I can't believe her. She amazes me.

She drops the loop over my head and shoulders,

and tugs it tight, pinning my arms to my body." Come here, city boy. I want to show you a few of my country tricks." She pulls me onto the bed and removes the lasso. I think she might want to keep going with her scheme for control, but I don't give her a chance. I gently shove her onto the bed and pin her body down with mine.

She pouts." I wanted to play lasso the cowboy."

"As you have aptly pointed out, I am a city slicker." I kiss her hard.

"You've on too many clothes," she protests between kisses.

"That I can remedy, but you have to promise to stay put."

"I promise."

I strip as fast as I can because I don't trust the little minx to do as she's told." I do have a few rope tricks of my own." I pick up the rope and loop it through my hands. I stand beside the bed, she's on her knees on the soft mattress.

I place one finger under her chin. "You're already soaked aren't you?"

She looks up as me, licks her lips, and nods.

"Raise your arms." She does as she's told. I slide the rope down around her hips and then further wind it around her wrists." Lay down."

She obeys, and I tie her arms to the headboard." Every time you move your hips, the rope will tighten around your waist."

She wiggles, and gasps as the rope also obeys my plans. "That's not fair. I wanted to tie you up."

I know she's turned on because her skin is flushed, and her blues eyes are black with desire. I spread her legs wide." Are you sure you don't want a safe word?"

She lifts her head to look at me and licks her lips." Bring it on, city boy."

"I will bring it. I'll bring you so close to heaven, you're going to beg me to let you go into the light."

* * *

I BROUGHT us both to heaven multiple times through the night, but when we finally fell asleep, it seemed like morning came way too early. There's been so much going on in my personal life, that for once I've let myself get way behind at work. My normally pristine office is full of stacks of paper and incomplete to-do lists.

I untangle from the sheets, and from Nash herself, and slip on a pair of jeans. It's only six in the morning, so Stella hasn't made coffee, so my caffeine craving will have to wait. She will not let me touch the coffee maker. The last time I did, it was a disaster.

I ignore the mess as I enter my office, even though the site of anything out of place usually makes my OCD go crazy. *It's Nash,* I think, smiling. *She calms me down.* I lean back in my leather chair and turn on my computer. I haven't answered many emails this week. There are hundreds of messages waiting for me. Most of them are not really important, just people cc'ing me on decisions they have the authority to make, but all my employees are fully aware that I insist on being kept in the loop about the smallest developments at Rylan Designs. They know I read every message I receive at some point, no matter how insignificant the matter may seem. One subject line jumps out at me, between meeting agendas and a funding request from the marketing department.

"Time for payback."

My stomach drops as I open it. Pictures of Nash and Anna skinny dipping in the pool pop up. There are even a few of Nash sleeping in our bed. At the end it says:

"If you think this is good, I've more interesting pictures for you."

There are no demands. Nothing. Shit. What the hell is this? I call Wayne.

He sounds groggy." Yes, Mr. Rylan."

I know I woke him, but I'm furious." I'm forwarding you an email I received. You need to beef up my security and find out how the hell someone got inside my house and took these pictures. And you need to find out who the hell it is. I want this information ASAP, like yesterday!"

Breathe. Breathe. Breathe. I can't tell Nash about the pictures.

"Yes, Mr. —"

"Put a security team on Nash, but tell them to stay out of her sight." I hang up before he has time to respond.

I send Nash a text, letting her know I'm going to my office in Moab. I need to do some more digging, and I can't risk her looking over my shoulder and seeing those photos.

CHAPTER SIXTEEN

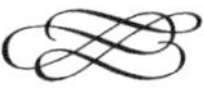

NASH

The bed is empty next to me, but I smell August on the sheets. I touch the redness on my wrist from the ropes he used on me in our latest lovemaking session. I blush thinking about it. He warned me to stay still, but I couldn't. The way he touched me was sweet torture. I can't believe how August awakens my senses. I never could've imagined I'd enjoy those kinds of escapades, and he makes me actually crave them.

I take a quick shower, slip on a sundress, and admire my new bracelet. The idea that I've captured his heart warms mine. He could have any woman in the world, but he chose me. I feel like I should do something special for him. He texted that he'll be at the Moab office, and I've never been there. I doubt he's eating enough, because once he gets sucked into work, he thinks about nothing else. A picnic would be a nice surprise, but I need to make sure Tom is taken care of before I even think about leaving. I relive the night aide and ask the daytime aide to give me a few minutes alone to assess Tom.

"Good morning, Tom," I say.

He smiles his crooked smile at me and blinks furiously. I wonder if that's his way of saying, *I'm so glad to see you, but where have you been?*

I put the stethoscope on his chest. "I'm sorry I haven't been around these past couple weeks. I had some personal matters to deal with." *That's the truth.* I smile at him. "Today is the day. I'm going to bring August in here later so he can see the progress we've been making." He reaches over to the nightstand and hands me the journal. I flip through the first few pages, but they're still blank.

"Augie," he says.

"Yes, August will be here today." He says something else, but I don't understand him." I'm not sure what you're saying." I pat his arm and the bracelet slips from under my sleeve. It's sparkling stone catches his eye. I dangle it before him." August told me I have his heart."

He smiles and nods, and then closes his eyes. It's amazing how these simple interactions exhaust him.

I enlist Stella to help me pack up a picnic. We put together a feast of sandwiches and fresh fruit and Stella's delicious homemade potato salad. I select a bottle of red wine, so I don't have to worry about keeping it cold. I'm excited about my plan, and I hope August will be excited, too. I hope he doesn't get mad at me for leaving the estate. I know he wants me to be safe, but I'm not going to be a prisoner here. He has to understand that. What could be dangerous about planning a picnic?

I drag all the stuff for lunch, complete with blanket and cloth napkins and a cooler of lemonade, out onto the front step. For a moment I'm confused because my car is gone. There's Fred, standing beside some sporty looking silver number. The car is so shiny, I put on my sunglasses as I approach it. I can see my own reflection, and the sparkling water from the fountain reflected in its sleek lines.

Before I can open my mouth to ask after the whereabouts of my Mustang, Fred starts talking. "Mr. Rylan had me take it to the shop for some much-needed repair work. He said to teach you how to use this one."

"This thing? Is this one of August's designs?"

"Yes. It's fully automated."

I walk around and open the driver's door." You mean it drives itself?"

"Yes, ma'am. Mr. Rylan instructed me to teach you how to use it."

"I don't know. Maybe you could just drive me to his office." I'm nervous about taking one of August's cars. I can't imagine what it's worth. What if I screw up giving the damn car instructions and it drives us into a brick wall?

He opens the door wider." It's very easy to operate."

Fred and I sit in the car and he launches into a detailed tutorial. He shows me how to map my course and all the other bells and whistles that come with this amazing vehicle. It's like something out of a science fiction movie. I wonder if the car has an actual mind of its own. Like maybe it will tell me when it doesn't like my outfit, or that I'm drinking too much coffee. It makes sense to me that August would want to build a car like this, something safe and predictable, after what happened to his parents.

"Okay," I tell Fred. "I think I can handle it." Fred gets out and waves me off. The car roars to life with the push of a button and drives itself through the gate. I find that I'm still sitting there, looking out the windshield, like I would in a traditional vehicle. The car tells me about my route and announces that traffic is all clear. It speaks in a calming English accent. It obeys the streetlights and speed limits all by itself. It plays my favorite music, and after I select a few songs, it figures out what I like, and sends a stream of popular country music tunes through the speakers.

The car parks in front of his office, a one-story stone building that blends into the surrounding countryside. I go inside, and the woman behind the front desk smiles at me. "I know who you are!" she says.

For a moment I'm not sure what to say. I've never seen her before.

"You're Mr. Rylan's girlfriend. He has a picture of the two of you beside his computer on his desk."

"Oh!" That seems sweet to me and makes me happier I came to surprise him. "Yes. I'm Nashville."

"You go ahead up. His office is the one at the end of the hall." She smiles. "The big one, of course."

I run up the stairs, and she's right, there's a double door at the end of the hallway that must lead to August's office. I knock, but I open it without giving him a chance to answer it. "Hey!" I say. "Surprise! I wanted to—"

He's hugging someone, and my heart falls as I recognize her. It's the dark haired woman who had placed her card in August's pocket at the party.

He steps away from her and walks toward me." Um...you remember Lisa?"

I don't say anything. I'm not sure what to say. I take in her chic dress and perfectly manicured fingernails. Her elegant shoes and tasteful makeup.

"Thank you for meeting with me, August." Her voice cracks as she says his name. I wonder if she's angry, or feeling guilty because I broke up their rendezvous. Her heels clickety-clack on the polished marble floor as she leaves.

"What are you doing here?" he asks me.

"Is that really what you want to say to me right now?"

"It's not what you think."

"Then tell me what it is. I came here to surprise you with a lunch, and I find you in another woman's arms. What the hell am I supposed to think?"

He tries to touch me, but I back up. His arms fall to his sides. "She came here because I wouldn't answer her phone calls."

"So you hug her?"

"She was hugging me. She was telling me goodbye. I didn't realize she had feelings for me, but I guess she did. That was part of the deal through the club. No attachments. I told her I had no feelings for her romantically and she was upset. She wanted more, and I told her about you."

"And how did she react to that?"

"She said she wished I had those feelings for her instead."

"That simple. End of story."

"It is for me. I'll never see her again." He reaches for me. This time, I let him pull me close.

"I don't understand how you can have sex with a woman and have no feelings for her? I've never been able to separate the two."

"All you need to know is that all of that ended the day I met you. I don't think I could separate the two now either." He lifts my chin so I have to look into his eyes." But know this, I don't ever want to meet any man who has had his hands on your body. I don't ever want to be in the same place with someone you had feelings for."

"I've never felt for a man the way I feel for you." I kiss him softly.

"What did you pack for lunch? I admit, I'm starving."

"For food or for me?"

"I'm always starved for you, but I skipped breakfast. A man needs nutrition if he's going to keep up with your sexual appetite." He kisses the top of my head.

We collect the picnic fixings from the silver car and set up beside the stream that runs behind his office. The breeze is heavenly, and there's a light smell of wildflowers in the air.

"This is beautiful," I say. "Your office is nice, but I would spend my entire day out here."

"Then I'd never get any work done. I'd daydream, or fall asleep." He smiles as I lay out the food. "What a spread!"

"I might have had a little help from Stella."

He takes a huge bite of his sandwich, chews, and then shovels some potato salad into his mouth. He coughs, and once I know he's not choking, I laugh." You really are starving."

"It was all that sex last night. You wore me out. So how do you like your new car?"

"What? Fred said you sent my car in for repairs." I stop eating.

"That's partly true. It needs to be fixed up some before you can sell it."

"I can't afford a new car. I'm just now starting to make a little headway on my student loans."

"I can afford it. I want you to have it. I want you safe."

I put my plate down." We have been through this a million times. I do not want or need you to buy me things. My car is perfectly fine."

He places his plate on the blanket and scoots toward me until our knees are touching." You need to understand that I will spend my money as I see fit. Your safety is of the utmost importance to me. The car is one way that I can see to it that nothing happens to you."

How do I make him understand that I just don't want him to have so much control over me? I know his motives behind the car are good, but it still makes me uncomfortable. Still, we're just starting to work through our problems. I really don't want to fight. I make a quick decision to choose my battles, and I do not choose this battle in this moment.

"Okay, well then, thank you." I touch his chin.

He squints at me." That was too easy."

"I will graciously accept your gift, but in the

future, please discuss it with me before you buy me anything."

"I'll try," he says.

It's a start.

* * *

We finish eating and I gather up the blanket." What time are you coming home?" I ask as we walk hand in hand back into his office.

"I have a few more things to do around here. Why? What did you have in mind?"

"And you think I have an insatiable sexual appetite." I laugh at him." I really want you to see your father's progress."

"I'll be home in a couple hours, but I'd rather see what progress I can make getting you out of those clothes." His mouth traces my jawline.

"You truly are *insatiable*." I kiss him, hard. The man just touches me, and I'm turned on.

He abruptly unlocks our lips." Not here. I want to finish this work stuff, so it's not on my mind when I want other things on my mind." He pinches my bottom and walks me to the car. When I sit in what should be the driver's seat, he tells the car to buckle my seatbelt, and it does.

"Now that's a neat trick," I say.

"Safety first." He smiles." I'll meet you back home in a few hours." He looks over his shoulder.

"Who are you looking for? The boogieman?"

He laughs, but his eyes are still serious. "Maybe."

* * *

TRUE TO HIS WORD, a few hours later he walks through the door. He is on the phone with someone and he sounds a little angry.

"Everything okay?" I ask as he says goodbye.

"Nothing for you to worry about." He kisses me.

"Come on. Let's go see your father." I take his hand and lead him up the stairs.

Tom is sitting in the chair with his usual blank stare. The one he presents to everyone but me. I ask the aide to leave, and I walk over to Tom. I kneel in front of him. August stands behind me.

"It's okay, Tom. I brought August with me to see how well you are doing." His stare remains fixed. I touch his hand." Don't worry. We're all in this

together."

Nothing.

"Tom, look at me."

Still nothing.

I can't believe Tom is doing this. I glare at him. "Why won't you cooperate?"

I feel August hand on my shoulder." It's okay, Nash."

I stand up." No, it's not. I swear to you that he interacts with me. He can even say a few words. He says your name." I turn to Tom." Say his name. Your son's name."

Nothing.

"That's enough. Let's go." August leads me out of the room." Don't worry about it, or be upset with him. He's been this way for years."

I pull my hand from his grasp." You don't believe me?"

"I believe you want him to talk. But baby, you're the only one who has ever said you see any kind of response from him."

"He does talk. He watches television, and he's even played cards with me."

"Okay. Okay, I believe you. But why doesn't he react to anyone else?"

"I don't know. This is so damn frustrating. I think he's hiding from you."

"That makes no sense." He holds me to him.

"I don't know." I start to cry.

"It's okay, baby." He pulls me close. "We can try again later."

"I'm exhausted,"I say between sobs." Maybe I'm coming down with something. It's not like me to cry."

"The flu bug has been going around. How about I go tuck you in bed and have Stella bring you up some hot tea?"

I nod. My head hurts, and so does my heart. I don't know why Tom won't talk to August. To his own son. But he'll talk to me. And August doesn't even seem bothered by it. Men make no sense to me.

CHAPTER SEVENTEEN

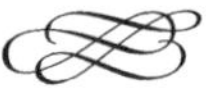

AUGUST

After a week, Nash is finally starting to feel like her old self. She had a nasty case of the flu. I know she's feeling better because she wakes me up by stroking me.

"Good morning. I've missed you." She says as she runs her tongue along my ear.

"Are you sure you're up to this?" I hope her answer is yes because my cock is aching to be inside of her.

She climbs on top of me after lowering my shorts." I'm more than ready. Besides, I want to take care of you, like you've taken care of me this week." She kisses the tip of my cock.

She puts me in her mouth. She starts out slow and

sweet, and her eyes get darker and darker with each suck. I breathe deeply and let her have her way. Just as I start to lose control she stops. She lifts her hips and slowly lowers herself onto my cock. She's so tight and so wet. I watch, enthralled, as she makes love to me.

* * *

After our shower, we enjoy a late breakfast together." I need to go into the office today for a conference call."

"Are you going to Seattle this week?" she asks.

"No." I don't offer any other explanation, and she doesn't ask, but the truth is, I haven't wanted to leave her. Wayne still hasn't been able to figure out exactly how the intruder got into my house. I'm not leaving Nash alone in this place with only Stella and an apparently faulty security system to protect her. "I'll be gone most of the day."

"It's okay. Anna and I had planned a Saturday shopping trip."

I fish a credit card from my wallet." Can you do me a favor and buy some sexy nightgowns?"

She shakes her head." I have my own money, thank you very much. But I'll see what I can come up with." She hops down from the barstool and kisses my lips.

"You are one stubborn woman."

"We're not getting into this fight this morning. I feel great for the first time in a week. I am not starting off in an endless argument with you." She grabs her purse. "An argument you know you'll never win."

I laugh. "I love you, Nash."

She kisses me again." Thank you for this morning."

"What do you mean?"

She blushes. "You know. Letting me take charge. I know how hard it is for you to let me have control."

I smack her on the ass. She laughs and rubs her bottom. It's like a silent reminder between the two of us. I love how she dominated me this morning, but that's not going to be the case very often. We both know who is in charge in the bedroom, and we both like it that way.

* * *

The conference call lasts over two hours, and by the time I hang up, I'm annoyed and tired. The entire call focused on haggling over the salaries of a few of my international vice presidents of operations. If one gets a raise, another wants one. If one gets a new bonus structure, I'm supposed to give it to all of them. No matter what's happening in the global markets. Then I had the board yammering away in the background. All this political maneuvering in my own company drives me nuts. I finally told them all I'd make the decisions myself, and they'd be final, and I didn't want to hear any more whining about it. Maybe not the most diplomatic approach, but I get things done.

I just want to get home to Nash. Everything feels simpler when I'm with her. As I stand to shove some papers and books into my briefcase, I notice a bulky envelope on my chair. I never sit while I'm on the phone— I pace around the room. So I didn't see it until now. It's addressed to me personally.

How weird, I think. I wonder how it got here. Usually, my assistant goes through my correspondence, or at least lets me know if something like this shows up.

I rip open the package. A note and several photographs land on my desk. My stomach drops as I look at the pictures. Photos of my dad and Nashville, by the lake on my property. He's in his wheelchair, and Nash appears to be talking to him. To my surprise, in one picture, his hand is in midair. He's throwing bread to the ducks. Nash wasn't imagining things. He is interactive.

I unfold the note with trembling hands. The handwriting is messy but perfectly legible.

I KNEW HE WAS ALIVE. You bastard. The two of you took too much from me. You WILL pay. You can keep your dirty money. It's too late for that.

I shake the envelope, and the shreds of a torn up check float down onto the desk. Whoever wrote this was right—I was trying to buy them off. I recently sent money to the family of the "victim" in my dad's second car accident, in the hope that they'd leave me, and hence Nash, alone.

I grab my hair and clench my teeth. Nash might not realize it, but she's ruined everything. If this guy discloses those pictures, and the world realizes my father is still alive, I'll be ruined.

I call Wayne, and I'm so agitated, I'm almost screaming into the phone. "I need my house on lock down. Nobody comes or goes without my knowledge. Do you understand me?"

"Yes, Mr. Rylan."

I tell him about the pictures." You need to find out how this asshole is getting onto my property."

"I'm working on a few leads, sir."

I feel the urge to scream at him. How can he be so calm? I end the conversation before it can go south. The last thing I need is Wayne quitting on me. He's having trouble with this conundrum, but I know he's one of the best security professionals in the country. I call Nash. She'll calm me down.

"Hey baby," she says.

Unfortunately, her sweet voice doesn't have the effect I'm hoping it will have. I'm too worked up about the potential disaster I have on my hands." Why did you take my father outside the house?"

"Uh, hello to you, too. I took him outside for some fresh air. Once. What's the big deal? And how do you know about it, anyway?"

"Someone took pictures of the two of you. Now there's proof that my father is alive. Floating around God knows where. Probably on the Internet."

"I'm sorry. I didn't realize—"

"You took him outside without my permission!"

"I wasn't aware I needed your permission. You told me to take care of your father. So that's what I did. The man needed a change of venue. It's not good for anyone, being locked up in your castle day and night!"

"Guess what? He's no longer your concern."

"Let me get this straight. You're firing me for taking your dad outside to get some fresh air?"

"You have no idea what you've done. The wrong people knowing that my father is alive could ruin me."

"Well, maybe it's time for you to face the music!"

"Why do you feel the need to fix things that aren't broken? Everything was fine just as it was!"

"Your father feels the need to hide from you, he won't communicate or even engage with anyone but me. He's hiding out in plain sight. Inside his own body. And you think things were fine?" She's yelling now, too.

"Did you ever stop to think that I don't want the bastard to speak again? You have no idea how he treated me. I'm happier with this version of him."

"August." I can tell she's trying to stay calm. "Your father loves you. I know he does."

I feel like she's talking to me as if I'm still eight years old. I don't want to prove her right by having a complete temper tantrum, so I try to get a grip on my own emotions. "Look, we can talk about this when I get home. I need some time to cool off. No one is to leave the house until further notice."

Silence.

"Do you understand me, Nash? I don't want to fight you about this. I need you safe."

"Yes. Of course. Your wish is my command." She hangs up the phone.

I wonder if she'll really stay put. Damn it. My mind goes into damage control mode. If this gets out, how am I going to spin the story? By the time my father had his stroke, his reputation was terrible. His own employees and board members hated him and had zero confidence in his abilities. I had to build my own reputation from the ground up and separate myself from him. Now everything I've worked for hangs in the balance. My heart knows it's not Nash's fault, but at the same time, I didn't have these complications when I didn't have anyone significant in my life. It just reminds me, I was a loner all those years for a reason.

CHAPTER EIGHTEEN

NASH

I stare at the phone after I hang up on August. What an asshole. All my efforts to heal the wounds between him and his father and all he cares about is protecting whatever business reputation he's built for himself. Even if that reputation is based on lies and secrets. I feel my own heart breaking, but I know I can't tie myself to someone who would make money more important than family. Even if his father was an asshole, I can't ignore how August himself is behaving. It takes one to know one.

I ruminate as I pack some essentials. I'll go to Anna's again. I at least need some time to think, away from August. Anna herself will probably think I'm nuts. All this back and forth? It's exhausting. I should've stayed away from him after I left him the first time. But when he showed up at my parents' house, and he seemed so sincere...

A crash from upstairs distracts me. I walk to the hallway and listen, but I don't hear anything else. Maybe I'm imaging things. I'm so distraught, and August's paranoia is rubbing off on me. I start back to the bedroom but decide I should at least check on Tom. Maybe an aide knocked something over. Or maybe Tom himself was trying to move or needed something. I walk upstairs, and to my surprise, the door is wide open. August likes it to be shut, and the staff knows that.

I peer around the corner and into the room. The aide is laying on the floor, not moving. A man, dressed all in black, stands over Tom with a pillow pressed to his face. Tom's arm flails in a weak attempt to push him off.

I run to the stranger and shove him. "Stop it!" I scream as I push him backward. He stumbles, probably out of surprise more than my great strength, and then grabs me. I struggle, and we both hit the ground. He pins my arms above my head.

"I could've killed him and walked out. Now I have to take care of you, too!"

The air is knocked out of me when Tom rolls off

the bed and lands on the assailant, who is on top of me. Tom is dead weight. The man in black flails and rolls around, and as he pushes Tom off himself, I'm able to squirm out from under him. I scramble to my feet, grab a bedside lamp, and knock the man upside the head with it. He falls to his knees, and I grab Tom. I try to drag him away. His eyes are on me, totally aware, and he's moaning. "Go. Go," he says.

"I'm not leaving you," I say.

But the man in black is faster and stronger than me. As I try to drag Tom toward the door. He shoves me backward. I lose my grip on Tom's wrists and slide across the floor on my butt. My tailbone explodes in pain. The man hits Tom in the head, three times, with the lamp. Blood flies across the room and hits the white sheets, the white walls, everything around us is red and white.

Tom's body twitches and spasms, and I know what that means. The man turns toward me. I can clearly see his face—a scruffy beard, small, angry blue eyes. All I can think about it the fact that if he's staring at me, and I know what he looks like, he's not going to let me live to tell this tale.

He swings the lamp in my direction. Pain on the side of my head, and then the world goes dark.

. . .

Two hours later

I TAKE some time to cool down, and the more I think about it, the worse I feel for yelling at Nash. She's only been trying to help, and in the end, so what if people know about my dad? I've spent years building a reputation on my own merit. Maybe she's right, and I have to put the past behind me and own my own reality. Nash really had no idea what was at stake, anyway. I told her no one could know about her work with my father, but I never explained what would probably happen if someone did find out. I never told her she shouldn't take him outside. Honestly, I wouldn't have thought to tell her that, because who would have believed she'd make so much progress with him anyway? That she'd get him to the point where he'd actually enjoy the sunshine, and feeding the damn ducks? I try to call her on the way home to apologize, but she doesn't answer.

I pull up to the front gate, but the guard isn't there. I buzz myself in and call Wayne at the same time.

"There's no guard at the gate," I say.

"I was just about to call you, sir. That guard—we just found out he's connected to the family that of the young man that died in that accident. His brother and that young man were good friends. He must be letting people onto the property. He's probably giving them information."

"What the fuck," I say. "Call 911. I have no idea what I'm walking into right now."

"Sir—be careful—"

I hang up. All I can think about is Nashville, in that house, with some crazy person after her. I drive up to the house and jump out of my car. I keep a gun in a safe in the garage. I grip the loaded weapon in one sweaty hand as I open the back door to the kitchen. I hear a rustling noise, and moaning. Stella is gagged and tied to a chair. Her panicked eyes meet mine, and I put my finger to my lips to quiet her.

I pull the gag out of her mouth." Where is Nash?" I whisper.

"I don't know." She's crying. "I heard the struggle, but I haven't heard anything in about an hour."

I loosen her hands. "Wayne called 911. I want you to lock yourself in the pantry until they get here. I'm going upstairs to look for her."

"Shouldn't you wait for the police?"

"No. I might already be too late." I shut the pantry door behind her.

I creep upstairs to our bedroom. There's a suitcase on the bed, but there is no sign of Nash. I whisper her name as I check closets and under the bed. I check the guest room, and there's nothing and no one in there. I'm terrified of what I'll find in my father's room.

The reality of the carnage is as bad as I expect. My father is dead, a pool of blood on the floor around his head. The aide is on the floor across the room. I check her pulse. She's still breathing. No sign of Nash.

My heart is in my throat as I lean down to close my father's eyes. They're already fixed, staring at the ceiling. His mouth hangs open as if he's finally about to speak to me after all these years. Something shiny in his hand catches my eye.

My heart stops. It's Nash's bracelet. I slip the bracelet into my pocket and call out to her, softly, even though I know she's not here. I straighten up and call for her louder. Still no answer.

It's my worst nightmare. He's taken her. Where, or why, I have no idea. But she's finally truly out of my control, and under the power of someone else. Someone whose intentions are terrible.

SIRENS ANNOUNCE the police's arrival. They search the house, and then I join them at the police station. We spent five hours discussing the details of the intrusion. I don't hold back—I tell them everything. Everything they could possibly need to know in order to find her.

When they finally have everything they need, I meet Wayne outside the station, beside my limo. "Tell me what you know," I say to him.

"The guard—the one who knew the family—he's been sneaking the father onto your property. The father of the guy who went over the bridge. They've been messing with the cameras, too."

"How about the men that were tailing Nash? Did they see anything?"

"No. They're tracking down that guard now to see what information we can get out of him." Wayne eyeballs the police officers as they approach their cruisers. "We have ways to get information out of people. Our own ways. The police might be too squeamish, but I'm not, and neither are my men."

"We have to find Nash."

"If this guy wanted to kill her, at least right away, he would have left her there, dead. I think this is a mind game against you, sir."

. . .

"I AGREE," I say.

"Do you want me to notify the girl's parents' sir?"

"No. Let's find her first.

* * *

THE GUARD LIVES thirty minutes outside of town, in a small rundown house surrounded by a rusty chain-link fence. There are a few houses around it, on a dead end street. I ask Wayne to have his men park a couple miles down the road and await my instructions. I want to check the place out first myself.

Fred pulls off on a side road and Wayne and I arm ourselves." You stay in the front. I'll go around to the back of the house."

The backyard is in even worse shape than the front yard. The windows are broken, and trash and old tires and other car components dot the patchy dirt and grass that leads to a ramshackle shed. I crouch by the back door, listening for Wayne to knock out front. Someone scrabbles around inside the house, and the back door flies open. The guard sees me and my drawn weapon and stops with his hands in the air. Wayne walks up behind the guard and cocks his own gun beside the man's head.

I creep in close to the man's face. "Where is she?"

"I don't know." He looks terrified.

"You have to the count of five to tell me where she is, or my friend here is going to put a bullet in your head."

"I swear I don't know where he took her. He told me he wasn't going to hurt anyone. He just wanted proof that your father was still alive."

"He did more than get proof. He killed my father, injured an employee, and took my girlfriend hostage!So if I were you, I would start thinking real hard."

"He has a cabin. A hunting cabin. It's two hours northeast of here. Up in the mountains."

Sirens peel out in the distance, and a cavalcade of police vehicles speeds down the dirt road. I see a few of the disheveled neighbors wondering their own patchy yards and peeking through mobile home windows. This is the most excitement they've had in years.

One of the officers comes around the house. His eyes widen when he sees me. "Lower your gun, Mr. Rylan."

I follow his advice.

"We're taking him into custody," the cop says.

I lean into the guard's ear." If you want anyway out of this mess, you better tell me exactly where I can find this cabin."

He whispers the address in my ear as the police cuff his hands behind his back.

* * *

I HAVE a hotspot in my limo, so we pull up a visual of the cabin and the surrounding area. It's heavily wooded and very secluded.

"What do you want me to do about the media, sir? They're already all over this. The Seattle office is in a frenzy. Three board members have already turned in their resignations. Northwest Industries and Cybertech have put their orders on hold.

I start to ask who quit the board, but honestly, I can probably guess. And who really cares, anyway, with Nash out there somewhere, in danger?" I can't think about the business right now. Once I have Nash back, I can focus on all that." I pause for a moment." Where did they take my dad's body?"

"He's at the morgue, sir. You'll have to go down there and ID him in order to get the body released."

"How is the aide that was injured?"

"She took a good hit to the head, but she'll be okay."

"And Stella?" I rub my hand down my face.

"She's shaken up, understandably, but not hurt. The guy obviously overpowered her. She didn't have a chance."

"Who roughs up a middle-aged housekeeper? And then my father... and Nash. I'll fucking kill this asshole."

"Sir, we should really let the police handle this."

"I'm not waiting around for them to fuck this up. I can't risk Nash."

Fred interrupts." We should be at the bottom of the mountain in ten minutes, sir. Do you want me to drive up?"

"No, park at the bottom. I want to surprise this mother fucker." I grit my teeth. "Maybe he's like me. Maybe he doesn't like surprises, but he's got one coming to him."

CHAPTER NINETEEN

NASH

My head is throbbing. I'm freezing. The air around me is heavy and musty. It makes my stomach turn, but I wonder if my nausea is related to the blow I took to my head. My right eye is swollen shut, and the coppery taste of blood is in the back of my throat. I can tell I'm bound with some kind of rope, so I can't move. It's dark. I kick my legs and hit solid walls. Maybe I'm in a closet.

I have no idea how long I've been in here. I can't see the walls, but it feels like they're closing in on me. I think about Tom, and I'm sure he's dead. Tears well up in my eyes, and I struggle with the ropes.

I rub my face against my bent knees. Falling

apart isn't going to help the situation. I have to calm down and think. The crack under the door fills with light, and the door opens. At first, I can't see. My right eye is swollen shut, and my left eye doesn't have time to adjust to the light. Someone roughly tugs me to my feet, and half drags me to a wooden chair. I blink, and the world comes into focus. I stare into the man's face. His same angry, beady blue eyes. He's still wearing the same black clothes. I'm sure they're splattered in Tom's blood, but it doesn't show up. Not like it did on the white sheets. That image will haunt my nightmares.

"Who are you?" I ask. It's a croak, from thirst and lack of use of my voice.

He places a water bottle to my lips. "Drink."

I hate doing what he says, but my body needs fluids. I gulp down water until he jerks the bottle away from me. Water dribbles down my chin. My shirt is soaked. *What a waste*, I think.

"Who are you?" I ask again.

"Tom Rylan killed my son. My son, Luke. Tom was on a drunken binge when my son's car went over that bridge." He has tears in his eyes.

I don't dare tell him that's not the story that I was told." I'm sorry you lost your son."

"August Rylan was never sorry. All he did was lie. He hid his father all these years. Neither of them ever faced what they did."

"You have your revenge. Tom is dead. What do you want from me?" My voice is strong, but I'm trying not to cry.

He runs his hand down my cheek, and my stomach turns.

"You're an unexpected bonus. I've been watching you." He stands behind me and presses himself against me. "I especially enjoyed the pool night. You have a remarkable body." He runs his lips along my ear.

I focus on my breathing to keep from gagging.

"I'm sure it would kill him to know that I touched you. Pretty boy Rylan's cute little toy."

"Keep your fucking hands off of me!" I squirm, and the chair almost tips over.

He reappears in front of me." You seem to be forgetting who is in control here."

I bite my tongue to keep from antagonizing him.

"Do you know he thought he could pay me off? After I sent him the pictures of you and your friend naked in the pool, he sent me a check for five million dollars. A few years ago I probably would've taken his money, but it's too late for that now. I know I can hurt him more by revealing him for the slime ball he is. His reputation will be as bad as his father's. Probably worse. Pretty boy will be penniless."

He leans down to untie my legs." I *am* curious. Which will cause him more pain? Losing his livelihood, or his woman?" He smiles.

"I'm not his girlfriend. I was leaving him. I caught him in one of his lies. One of many. Killing me might wound his pride, but he only truly cares about his money." I try to sound like I mean it. Deep down, August would go off the deep end if I died.

I pull at the bonds on my wrists. The rope gives a little. The creepy man in black unwinds the rope from around my legs. His hands slide up and down my calf. There's a gruesome smile on his lips, and I know he's enjoying torturing me. My skin is crawling at his touch. I can't help it, my stomach leaps into my throat. He jumps away from me when I start retching. I gasp, trying to get control of my body. I spit on the floor in front of me.

He brings me a towel from the cabinet across the room. My eyes dart around the dark space. Dilapidated stairs lead up to a door. I'm in a basement. Tools hang off a peg board in the far corner of the room. The whole place is dimly lit by a single lightbulb. Exposed wires and pipes run the length of the ceiling, and an ancient hot water heater huddles in the corner. There's no other furniture, and the cement floors are bare.

He drops the towel in my lap, almost as a joke, since my hands are tied and I can't do anything about it. He doesn't say anything as he climbs the rickety stairs. He flicks off the light before he shuts the door. I'm in darkness again, save for the thin stream of light that slips under the basement door.

My thoughts go to August. My last words with him were harsh, and so were his to me, but I know he loves me. He must be frantic, trying to find me. Still, I can't wait on him. If I am going to survive, I'm going to have to save myself.

It takes at least an hour, but finally, through careful maneuvering, my hands are free. I rub the rope burn on my wrists and remember the layout of the room. I don't want to make any sudden moves and run into anything. I run my hands down the cold, dark walls until I hit the tools. I feel for the ax. It's heavy in my hands, but reassuringly so.

I curl up into a ball behind the stairs, so he won't be able to see me when he comes back. My breath comes in quick, anxious puffs, and I'm sure if there was enough light, I could see it in a fine mist around my face.

I'm at this man's mercy. All I can do now is wait. I wonder where August is, and if he's making any headway in finding me. Despite our fighting, I love that fucked up man. He owns my heart, but my head is telling me I can't live in his world. I'd never ask him to give it up. He might be afraid he'll lose everything, but he's too smart and hard working for that. And besides, since he's taken over Rylan Designs, he's maintained a pristine relationship with everyone involved in the company, and done so much good for the communities where he lives. He's a good, kind man. He's the product of his own tragedies like we all are. I wish he and Tom could've made amends. Still, no matter how much I love him and how good he is, this fancy, flashy, complicated life just isn't natural to me. I can't live like this forever. *Right now, I don't know if I'll even survive the night.*

Footsteps cross the floor above me, and the door creaks. I stand and brace myself. I grip the ax as if it's a baseball bat. Despite the cold, I'm sweating. The light comes on when the man in black is halfway down the stairs. He pauses, obviously confused when he sees the empty chair, and I swing. The ax hits his leg with a sickening thud that comes from hitting soft flesh and then meeting hard bone. He stumbles down the rest of the steps and lands on the concrete in a puddle of flailing arms and legs and splattering blood.

"You bitch!" He grips his leg. His shin is gushing blood through his ripped up black pants. I scurry around him, but he grabs my leg. I trip and drop the ax. I kick him once, twice, three times, and on the third blow, I connect with his chin. I scramble to my feet, run up the stairs, through the cabin's single room, and out the door.

It's almost dark out. Evening. It's just going to get darker, and all I can see around me is a dirt road lined with thick forest. I run to the car parked in the grass, but it is locked. Shit. If I stay on the dirt road he will find me.

I hear him yelling." I'm going to fucking kill you!" I take off running for the woods, but its hard to see where I'm going. It's getting darker by the second, and one of my eyes is out of commission. I hold my arms in front of me, trying to push the branches out of my way, least one poke me in my left eye and render me totally blind.

If I'm looking ahead I'm not looking down, and that spells disaster. I trip, maybe on a root, and plunge over the side of an embankment. My body gets another shock as cold water rushes over me. I've landed in some kind of river. I struggle to the surface and fight to keep my head above the rapids. It's all I can do to stay alive, but I take comfort in the fact that I can no longer hear the man in black screaming.

CHAPTER TWENTY

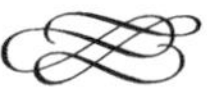

AUGUST

Wayne shines his light in the direction of the cabin. It's a ramshackle wood plank building with a skinny chimney. The front door is wide open and the lights are on inside." Stay low but be ready," Wayne says.

We walk past a parked car, some kind of older sedan. I shine my light in the back seat, and it's empty. My gun is cocked and ready as we clip across the gravel driveway. A light breeze blows leaves around our feet in the gathering darkness. We both pause as we step onto the rickety porch. The steps squeal beneath us, and I'm sure anyone inside this tiny place can hear us coming.

"Let's just go in," Wayne whispers. "Quickly."

My heart is pounding; I'm expecting a confrontation, but the cabin is empty. Ratty old furniture, a worn blanket, a few bags of chips and a half eaten Subway sandwich. Beers cans. And old Playboy pinup on the wall above a rusty stove. And more sinister—there are stains on the wooden floor. They look like blood. And it's not quite dried, so unless the occupant of this place likes to skin and butcher his deer right here in his little living room, I suspect that's human blood. We creep down the basement stairs. More blood, and in the middle of the room: a wooden chair covered in coils of rope. The bastard tied her up. Wayne opens a closet door, and for a moment I'm terrified of what he'll find. I'm relieved when the closet turns out to be empty.

"It's hard to see down here," I say, peering into the gloom. "Are there any more lights?" My foot strikes something hard. I look down, and to my shock, it's a bloody ax. "Oh my God. Nash."

Wayne rests a hand on my shoulder." Don't jump to conclusions yet, August. She may have broken free and used it on him. We need to keep looking for her."

I want to sit on the floor and cry, but I know that won't do Nash any good. I rub my eyes. "We need to call the police now. We need some help."

"No service out here."

"Keep trying while we search for her."

We search the rest of the cabin but come up with nothing. Wayne points to the trail of blood on the floor." I hate to say it, sir, with this much blood, I bet there's a trail we can follow outside, too."

We follow the splashes of blood. By flashlight, it looks dark brown, almost coppery. I wish I had a thicker coat. If Nash is out here, she has to be freezing. Guilt washes over me. My last words to her were so harsh. What if those really were our last words? I can't let myself think that way. *She's out here. Somewhere. She's hiding.*

The trail of blood stops abruptly at a steep embankment. I shine my light down the hill, and the leaves and dirt are churned up. It's possible someone slid down into the river.

The river. It's not that wide, but it's flowing fast, and I know it will be freezing. It's basically just melted snow coming down the mountain.

A human figure is wandering around the small rocky beach at the river's bend." Nash?" I stumble down the bank myself, running along an old log, so I avoid landing in the river. I jump onto the beach. Sand and gravel spray up around me. I already can tell it's not Nash. The person in front of me is too big and bulky.

"Where is she?"

"I'm sure she's dead by now." The kidnapper laughs. He slaps his hands on his thighs. It's all hilarious to him. *He's insane.*

I place the pistol to his forehead and he stops laughing. He holds up his hands. Wayne grabs my arm." Don't do it, August. If you kill him, he can't rot in jail."

I step back but keep the gun trained on his face. Wayne checks his phone." I have service here." He gives the dispatcher our location and asks for additional help with the search.

"You stay with this wacko," I say." Nash is a smart girl. She would head downstream to get off this mountain. I don't want you to leave his side until he's cuffed and in the back of an ambulance."

The kidnapper is sitting on the beach. He's rocking, and talking to himself. There's a dirty rag tied around his leg." She did this to me!"

Good girl." You are lucky she didn't do more damage. I would have killed you on the spot." He kicks at me with his good leg. That's the last straw for me. I punch him square in the jaw, and he's knocked out cold.

Wayne chuckles." Nice left you have there."

"I would love to stay here and beat the shit out of him, but I need to find Nash."

I walk along the embankment. It's so steep. The little beach is an anomaly. In most places, you'd either be on the embankment, or in water over your head. I call out for her. The whitewater is loud, but I'm louder. I walk for about twenty minutes. I'm grateful that the clouds have broken, and the moon is almost full. It provides light beyond the narrow beam of my flashlight.

I'm starting to panic. Time is clipping on, and I know that if she's out here, she's close to freezing to death. I stop and scream her name.

Something in the water is moving, and it's not just the rapids themselves. There's a flash of yellow.

Nash is clinging to a rock in the river. She's half in, half out of the water, and her yellow tee shirt is plastered to her skin.

I don't pause for a second. I jump into the water. It's so cold, my breath explodes out of my mouth as if my lungs themselves are protesting. I fight my way across the river. My feet can just touch the bottom in some places, so I have some control. Nash wouldn't have the same advantage—she's too short.

I reach her and wrap my arms around her. She's breathing, but she's not conscious. I drape myself over her, whispering, trying to warm her up with my own body heat.

It takes a few minutes, but she finally stirs. The color is returning to her lips." August," she says, faintly." You came."

"I'll always come for you."

"You were so angry with me."

My heart hurts at her words. "I'm so sorry, baby. I had no right to be angry with you." I kiss her lips lightly.

"Tom?"

I clench my eyes tight." He's gone."

She bites her lip, and I think she might start crying, but we have to focus on the task at hand." Don't think about him right now. I have to get you out of here." I need to get her back to the spot where I left Wayne. The police should be here by now.

The fight back across the river is exhausting, but we make it. Nash clings to my back. I choke and sputter my way through the rapids. My head is under water some of the time, but I make sure she stays above the rustling waves. Once we get up the embankment, I set her down for a moment to get my breath.

She sees how winded I am. "Let me walk."

"No. You're not strong enough."

"If you try to carry me along this embankment, and slip, we'll both go over the side." She gives me a tired smile. "Then you would've rescued me for nothing."

I pull her to her feet. "You make a good point, but you rescued yourself, Nash. I just came along at the end."

She is a little off balance, but she's right. It's easier to steady her than carry her. We lean on each other as we pick the safest path along the riverside. *This is how it should be, always,* I think. *Me and Nash, leaning on each other.*

I SEE blue lights flashing up in the distance." Wayne!" I yell. A beam of light from his flashlight hits me square in the face, blinding me. "Whoa," I say, as I stumble. I shake my head to clear my eyesight. Nash cries out in pain, and I'm reminded of her terribly injured eye. "Hey! The light. Get it out of our faces for now." I take her hand. "I got you, baby. Let me lead you."

There's a chopper spinning around above us.

"They already took the kidnapper," says Wayne.

"He's cuffed and secure. You two go ahead. I'll take the car back."

The chopper lowers a basket and hoists Nash to safety. Once she's inside, I follow her. I watch the river below me and think about how close she came to dying. At the hands of a lunatic, and at the mercy of nature. I shiver. I've learned a lesson. I'll never take her for granted again. I'll never speak to her like that, or allow petty arguments to separate us. I think of my father, now dead and gone. Never a chance to tell him how I really felt. Old hurts, old anger, kept us apart.

That'll never happen between me and Nash. Never.

THEY CHECK me out at the hospital, but I'm impatient. I know there's nothing wrong with me. Once they agree with me, they let me stay in Nash's room. Fred brings me some clothes, and Wayne is the one who goes to the police station to give the initial statement. The police agree to let me come in another day. I want to be here when Nash wakes up. The nurse brought me a pillow, so I dragged two chairs together and I'm trying to find a way to get comfortable. The yellow plastic cushions sure aren't as cozy as my ten-thousand-dollar mattress back home.

The nurse peeks in on us." Can I get you a cup of coffee, Mr. Rylan?"

"That'd be great thanks." I scruff my hand across my rough face. I'm gripping Nash's hand under the bedrail. My arm is falling asleep.

"August." Her hand moves in mine, and I forget the pins and needles.

"Hey, beautiful." I sit up straight.

"You must be blind."

"Your baby blue eyes are the most beautiful things I've seen in days." I kiss her nose. "Or, the baby blue of one of them. Haven't seen that one yet." I smile and point at her right eye. It's covered in a patch.

"Is it over? Is he dead?"

"It is over, but he's here in the hospital. He needed surgery from the blow you gave him." I feel her tense." Don't worry. He's handcuffed to a bed, under armed guard. He can't hurt you anymore."

"I thought he was going to kill me." She chokes on her tears.

"I promise it's over." I hold her to me as she cries. It's hard, with the stupid bedrail in between us and the awkward yellow chairs, but I do my best, and her sobs slowly taper off.

The nurse interrupts with the coffee." She's awake! I'll give you a minute, then I'll be back with the doctor."

"How is my eye?" Nash asks.

"It looks pretty bad, but the doctor said there's no permanent damage. You got six stitches in your chin. I'm just thankful that the majority of the blood trail was his, and not yours. I was scared to death when I saw the amount of blood in that basement. You did good, baby."

"I was so scared."

"I was, too."

She starts to cry again." I'm sorry I couldn't save your father."

"I saw how hard you tried."

"He tried to save me, too. I know you don't believe me. About him being able to communicate. But he rolled off the bed, right onto that lunatic. I wouldn't have gotten as far as I did without Tom's help."

I reach in my pants pocket." I know he did what he could." I hand her the bracelet. "He found a way to let me know that you were gone. For that, I'm very grateful."

The nurse and doctor ask me to step outside while he examines Nash. I've some time to kill, so I pay a visit to the kidnapper. The murderer. The lunatic who tried to turn our lives upside down. The guard stands as I enter the room.

"What the fuck do you want?" The crazy man glares at me and tugs at his cuffs.

"Walt." I spit out his name. He freezes. Maybe he didn't realize I knew his name. He'll always be the murderer, lunatic, kidnapper, to me, but he's Walter Palmer to the rest of the world." For once, you are going to shut your damn mouth and listen to me. My father was a lot of things, but he did not kill your son. The night of your son's accident my father was parked off the side of the road. Yes, he had been drinking, but he had enough sense to pull over. Your son, on the other hand, was wasted. The report shows he was high on heroin. He fell asleep at the wheel and swerved off the road. He hit my father's car and went over the embankment into the water."

"That's not true. He wasn't on drugs."

"I did some digging. You had that bit of information buried. Your son's history of drug addiction. In and out of rehab, right?"

Walt glares at me but says nothing.

"You wanted to blame someone, so you found

out my dad's history, and then you came after him, and came after me. You didn't leave me a lot of choices. I had to protect what was left of his reputation and I wasn't about to let you drag me down with him." I walk over to the rail of his bed." Despite what you've tried to do to me and the people I love, I'm still sorry about the loss of your son. Still, you killing my father and kidnapping my girlfriend is unforgivable. I feel sorry for you. I've made bad choices out of desperation. To cover for someone that I loved. I'll pay the consequences for my actions, whatever they may be. You'll lose your freedom for yours." I hear him crying as I leave his room.

I stop in the bathroom and wash my face before returning to Nash. I don't recognize myself in the mirror. For the first time in a long time, I'm looking into the face of a man that is unsure of himself. My financial future is on the line. I still have to go to the morgue to get my father's body released.

I wash my face a second time as if I can erase the haggard, anxious reflection in front of me. It doesn't work, so I towel off and return to Nash's room.

She's on the phone with her parents when I walk in. "I'll come home as soon as I can, Daddy. And yes, I will thank August for you for saving me. I love you, too." She hangs up." Momma was crying so hard she couldn't even speak to me."

"I wanted to be with you when you told them." I sit down beside her.

"I wanted the time to myself with them." She rubs the back of my hand.

"The doctor says I can go home today."

"I'll make all the arrangements. And make sure that Stella is stocked up on all your favorites."

"How are *you*? Really?" She stares into my eyes.

"Don't worry about me. You know I always have a plan. Today I have to worry about dad's body. I have to start planning his funeral."

She frowns at me." You don't seem sad."

"The man I remember as my dad has been gone a long time."

"Is it okay that I am sad for the both of you?"

"Of course," I say, and smile. "If being sad for us makes you happy, go ahead."

CHAPTER TWENTY ONE

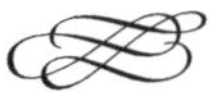

NASH

August spends the next week or so in Seattle, smoothing things over with his board, employees, and clients. I'm alone a lot. My body is healing, but it'll take longer for my mind to catch up with it.

I finally got the nerve to go back into Tom's room. August had everything cleaned out, so there's nothing but a box of personal stuff on the bed. The funeral was short and private and held in Seattle. I didn't attend, because I just didn't feel up to it. August didn't mind. He's been so businesslike about the whole thing. It's just hard for me to understand, being that I'm so close to my parents. He's been distant with everyone, even Stella. Even me. I know it will take some adjustment to get back to normal. I wish there was some way I could hurry it up.

The journal is in the box, so I take it. I gave it to him in the first place, and he never used it. So it seems like it should be mine.

I have to get out of the house, so I go to Sam and Claire's for dinner. Sam told me several funny stories about his escapades with August.

He's walking on his own and has been spending time with people his own age. He gets a phone call and excuses himself to take it.

"Maybe a girl," says Claire. "His confidence is growing every day."

"August would love seeing him doing so well."

"It's all thanks to August that Sam even has a chance at a normal life." She scoots closer to me. "Whatever his father did, August made up for it."

"I know, it's just sad because his father really did love him. August didn't get to see it. Sometimes I think he didn't want to see it. It was easier to hate him than try to forgive him."

"That relationship was very complicated for August. He's a complicated person."

"I don't know if I can ever fit in his world." The words are painful, but I have to say them.

"What are you talking about? You're the best

thing that has ever happened to him." Sam is back, and he sits beside me on the couch." He fell in love with you the minute he laid eyes on you. I've never seen August speechless around a woman. I've seen him be an asshole, but I've never seen him speechless."

"Sam! Watch your mouth," Claire says.

I laugh." It's okay, Claire, I've seen his asshole side too."

"Seriously, he does love you, Nash." Claire is adamant.

"It's not a question of love. His world is overwhelming to me. I like the simple things in life, and he likes the grander things. The drama that comes with him is too much sometimes."

"I don't think he has ever had anyone love him for just himself, at least in his mind. When we met him, we accepted what he could do for our lives. It wasn't until he let us into his life, that we loved him for himself, despite his money and power. He could have been dirt poor at that point and we would've still loved him. He's a good man that deserves to be loved by a woman like you."

Two weeks pass, and I have still barely spoken to August. He says there's too much going on in Seattle and he just can't make it home. I call Anna for a respite for my loneliness in this big house. She loves to visit August's house. I think it makes her feel swanky. So she's sitting beside me in less than an hour. I'm finally able to tell her the truth about everything.

"Oh my God. You almost died." She hugs me." I'm so sorry about all the things that have happened to you. You look awful by the way."

I slap her leg and laugh." Thanks a lot."

"No, seriously, you've lost weight. You look pale."

"Trust me, I'm not as pale as I was in the hospital. It's just taking me a little longer to recover than what I thought it would. I'm exhausted all the time. Naps have become part of my daily routine. Maybe some of it is just that I'm lonely and bored."

"I have the solution for that." She leaps to her feet. Her bouncing up and down nauseates me.

"What?"

"Let's book a cruise. The port is only a few hours away and Mexico will be fun this time of year."

"I don't know....

"Come on, it'll be a blast." She's all smiles.

"I'll talk to August about it." She hands me the phone. I set it in my lap. "I didn't mean right now."

"There's no time like the present. I'm ordering our tickets, so hurry up and call him."

I walk out onto the pool deck and call him. He answers on the second ring." What's wrong?"

"Well hello to you, too."

"I'm sorry, baby. You just caught me at a bad time."

"I just wanted to let you know that Anna and I are going on a quick cruise to Mexico this week."

"Okay, have fun."

"Wait, you don't want to discuss it and tell me that I can't go?"

"Is that what you want me to do?" He sounds confused.

"No, but that's what I'm used to with you. You always want to control my comings and goings."

"I'm sorry. I'm really caught up with things here. There's no reason for you to sit in that big lonely house, waiting for me to come home."

"You're right. I love you, August."

"I love you, too." He hangs up.

THE CRUISE with Anna is just what I need. I have color on my face again, and I gained a few pounds eating all that Mexican food. We swam with the stingrays and went on a dune buggy ride, and of course, we lounged around in hammocks, sipping fruity drinks and giggling. Since I'm in a better mood, I really can't wait to see August. He said he would be home for dinner tonight. Anna and I did a little shopping while we were gone. I bought a sexy little piece of lingerie that August will love.

I make it back in time to smell the heavenly meal Stella has been slaving over. She's all smiles when she sees me. She's as excited as I am to have August home.

"Welcome back, Nash." She throws her arms around my neck and kisses my cheeks.

"I don't know what smells so good in here, Stella, but I'm *so glad* to be home. Is August here yet?"

"He's been here for about an hour. I think he went upstairs to shower. Tell him dinner will be ready in thirty minutes." She yells as I skip out of the room.

I run up the stairs. It seems like it's been forever since I have seen him. It's been even longer since I've touched him.

I bounce into the room. He's just coming out of

the bathroom. He is toweling his hair and has another towel wrapped low around his waist, revealing his rock hard abs. The sight of him makes me instantly wet. I run into his arms.

"I am so glad you're home." I kiss him hard. His mouth parts and I explore him with my tongue. I feel him harden underneath the thin towel.

"I have missed you, too."

I don't know whether it has just been awhile since we have been together, but I am horny as hell. I want all of him, right here and now. I yank the towel from around his waist and take his hard cock in my hands.

He pulls back. "Not so fast baby. You're going to unman me in seconds."

"Sorry, I just want you so badly. It has been so long."

He walks me over to the bed." Come here and let me hold you for a minute."

I am a little disappointed, but I do as he asks." Mmm. You smell so good." I snuggle into his neck.

"Did you girls have a good time? You've a little color on your cheeks."

"It was exactly what I needed. Oh, I bought you something." I hop off the bed and grab a bag out of my suitcase. "Don't move, I'll be right back."

He laughs. "I thought the gift was for me?"

"Trust me. You're going to love it. Don't move an inch." I change and brush out my hair. I apply a light shade of lip color and some blush. I take one last look in the mirror and push my breast a little higher. He's going to love this. I open the door slightly and drape one leg out the door.

I hear him laugh. I open the door wide and rest my arms against the doorframe. I'm on full display for him now. He stops laughing. His mouth hangs open.

He stands up as I approach the bed. "This is a hot little number."

"You like?"

He walks behind me and places his hands on my breast. I pant at the contact. He sweetly kisses my shoulder and then bites at it. I inhale from the sting.

"Take if off," he says.

"But, I thought you'd like it." I try to turn but he doesn't allow it.

"I love it. I would just love it better on the floor." He nips at my ear.

"Oh." I feel that familiar throbbing, down low in my belly. He presses his erection into my backside and I groan. He pulls the hem of my gown up over my head. He pushes onto the bed. My ass is in the air. He lightly smacks me." I've missed this ass. I like it a little pink."

He flips me over and positions me so that my ass is on the edge of the bed. He parts my legs. He stares down at me. His cock is lengthening and hardening before my eyes. He kneels, and licks me." I've missed the taste of you. He has my moisture on his lips. It's such a turn on.

"Please."

My hands are in his hair. His tongue is magical, and my orgasm builds. He inserts two fingers inside me. I yank his hair.

"Come for me, baby," he says.

Done. Just like that, my body explodes. He continues to gently lick me until I come back to earth.

"Please. August, I want you inside me." My need for him is staggering.

"As you wish baby." He thrusts into me, hard. It pushes me along the bed until my head is hanging precariously off the side.

"Too much?" he asks.

"Again."

He slams into me three more times. We both fall off the bed, but somehow we manage to stay connected. I'm on top of him, but he's sitting up. His hands are on my ass and my nails are running down his back.

"Ride me, baby."

The lust in his eyes fuels my fire. I ride him just as hard as he was thrusting into me. He lets me bring us both pure pleasure.

After his own climax, we lay tangled on the floor. My feet are propped up on the bed and August lays between my legs. I can feel him breathing, and his body is covered in a light sheen of sweat. As I run my hands down his back, I feel raised areas. He has a few long scratches on his back. I guess I got a little carried away.

I rub them." I'm sorry."

He kisses my chin." You can mark me anytime. I'm all yours."

"I'm glad you're back."

He rolls off of me." Don't be too excited. I won't be here for long."

"Why, are things still crazy?"

"There's still a lot of backlash. I'm going to have to do damage control for a while to save the company." A dark cloud of stress seems to fall over him. It's so different from the lust I just saw in his eyes.

"Why don't you sell the company? You said

yourself that you have more than enough money." I rub his chest.

"Why would I want to sell the company?" He stands, abruptly. I'm left missing the warmth of his body.

I stand, too." The company doesn't make you who you are. Rylan Designs was built around secrets and lies. Why not start over with something else? Something that doesn't require you to work all the time. Something that will let you enjoy your life." We both get dressed as I talk.

"No way. I've spent my life building this. I'm not letting it go. I just don't want to sell it, frankly."

"What about what I want, August? I've tried to fit into your world, but you don't try very hard to fit into mine!"

He runs his hands through his hair." I don't have the time or the energy to fight with you about my life right now."

I feel as he just slapped me across the face." Excuse me? I thought we were trying to build a life *together*. It sounds to me like you want everything your way. I'm just supposed to sit back and wait for you to squeeze me in somewhere!"

"That's what I need from you right now. I'm on

the verge of losing my company. My father was murdered. I'm holding on by a thread!"

"And I was kidnapped by the insane man that murdered your father! Or are you forgetting that?"

"No. I haven't forgotten." His voice is a little softer. He walks toward me, but I take a step back.

"I'm sorry." He turns and walks out of the room.

As he disappears, I can feel my heart shattering into a million tiny pieces. I love this man with everything in me, but I can't do this anymore. His life is too complicated. I never thought I could love someone so much, but not be able to be with them. My life has been in a constant upheaval since I met him. I have to face reality. It's too tumultuous. Too many highs and lows. I just want stability.

I take the stairs slowly and purposefully, trying to prepare for what I know I need to do. He's already in his office, working. He glances up at me, then turns back to his computer.

"August, I love you, but I can't do this with you anymore."

He stops typing.

I rush on before I lose my nerve. "My life has been chaos since I met you. I've tried to help you, and mold myself to you, but you won't let me help you, and you won't give an inch. This is not the kind of relationship I want. I need a partner. Someone who can share himself completely with me, like I do with him."

He's still looking at the computer screen. My world shatters when he opens his mouth." You need to go then. I don't have time to have a partner. I've done fine all these years without one." He rises from his chair." I don't need someone to love me."

"Everyone needs someone to love them. I loved you!"

"Loved. Past tense." He stares at me.

"I do love you. I'd die for you if you could really give yourself to me. But I won't let myself die *because* of you." I leave the office. When I hit the stairs he finally calls after me.

"Nash."

I turn to look at him. He starts to say something, but instead, he turns back to his work.

CHAPTER TWENTY TWO

AUGUST

I was alone at my father's funeral. There was no one to mourn him. He had died years ago. I placed him to rest alongside my mother. Now I can visit both of them, together, like I'm doing right now. She loved him, so I'm sure she welcomed him with open arms. They're finally at peace together. Now my last link to her is gone.

The breeze picks up, and a few random flower petals from some other grave blow past their single headstone. I picture it as them walking off together, hand in hand. Following the petals. Light and graceful and full of hope. Leaving the pain of this world and their long separation behind them.

"Bye, Mom. Bye, Dad."

I drove the Jag, so I'm surprised when my limo pulls up next to it. What is Fred doing here? The door opens, and Claire gets out.

"I came to the office, but Margaret said you were probably here." She hugs me to her.

"What are you doing here?"

"I'm here for you. I don't want you to be alone."

Sam gets out of the car. He walks to me, slow and steady, and puts a hand on my shoulder. We walk back to my dad's grave. I stand in between them. These two people whose lives my dad almost ruined.

"I hated you for years," Sam says, staring at the headstone. "You took something away from me and my mom."

"Sam...."

"Let him finish." Claire takes my hand.

"But what you gave us in return was much more than you took away. You gave us August. So for that, I'm grateful." Sam wipes a tear.

"I don't know how, but your son is a good loving man," Claire says." I just wish we could ease the sadness and loneliness that has followed him for years."

"Thank you for giving him to us. I know he can be an ass, but he's our ass." Sam winks at me, and I'm amazed and proud to have been part of this young man's life.

* * *

Over the next several weeks, business slowly goes back to normal. I work overtime, calling and visiting everyone I know. Old clients. Potential clients. Former and current board members. My executive team. I travel to four countries to make sure I touch base with everyone who could have a negative effect on Rylan Designs. I reassure them that my father has been out of the picture for a long time. That I'm still in control, and everything is stable. Our plane and boat launch product launches go well, despite my worries about them. Maybe not quite as successful as they would have been before all this happened, but nowhere near the tragedy I feared. My hard work at keeping it all together seems to be paying off. Of course, nothing is together in my heart or my mind. So I bury myself in work. I can't stand thinking about Nash.

I pour myself a bourbon and watch the sun settle over Seattle from my office windows. I know she'd love this view—and the colors. Reds. Oranges. Tinges of pink and blue. *It doesn't matter if she'd love it. She's gone and I have to move on.* I gulp my drink and flip through my phone till I find the number of the secret club. The one that's just for sex, not strings. I call, but when the recording picks up, I hang up. I can't do it. I'm not ready. I'm not sure I'll ever be ready for meaningless sex again.

Damn her. I should've never let her in. Now I have to figure out how to live without her. I pushed her away, and then instead of stopping her, I literally helped her out the front door. The day she left, I carried her bags to the car. I know she wanted me to say something to make her stay. She told me if I ever needed her she was a phone call away. I need her every fucking night, yet I have never called her.

A MONTH later I finally make it back to Utah. The house is the same, but something is missing. Nash, of course.

"Welcome home Mr. Rylan. I have missed you." Stella kisses both of my cheeks.

"Thanks. It's good to see you too."

"Are you just visiting or are you staying for a while?"

"I'll be here for a few weeks. I promised Sam a climb and a camping trip."

I HEAD FOR THE STAIRS, but for some reason, I decide to stop in my father's bedroom first. The room is different. No more medicinal smells. No more beeping machinery or blinking lights. The metal bed-frame and mattress are still there, bare of sheets. All the pictures that Nash brought up are gone. I sit on the bed. I regret not listening to Nash about my father. Somehow, she connected with him in a way that I never have. Maybe I never let him. I wonder if he was trying, all those years, to reach me? I wonder if my anger and resentment made him too afraid to follow through?

"August." It's Stella." I've been standing in the door calling you."

Her use of my first name surprises me, but I'm too tired to tease her about it. "I'm sorry. I was lost in thought."

"This package just arrived for you." She hands it to me and sits down beside me.

It's a plain shipping envelope addressed to me. The return address says

N. Jacoby. My heart skips a beat.

"Aren't you going to open it?" Stella asks.

I lay it on the bed beside me." Not right now."

"But it's from Nash. It must be important."

"Okay. You're right." I open it. It's a journal. The one Nash left beside my dad for all those weeks. There's a note on it, in Nash's bubbly handwriting.

Dear August,

I took this with me when I left for a reminder. I didn't realize what treasures it held until I flipped through the pages. I hope this in some way helps you to heal and that it helps you decide, what's next, August?

Nash

Stella stands to leave." I'll let you read it alone." She kisses the top of my head.

I flip through the first couple of pages and they are empty, but something catches my eye. It's Nash's handwriting again.

. . .

I THOUGHT the journal was empty. Go to the middle of the book.

I OPEN it to the middle and I see shaky handwriting.

AUGIE,

I KNOW that you hate me for the things I have done to you. I can only tell you how sorry that I am and hope that one day you can forgive me. I couldn't stand to see the hate in your eyes for me. I do not blame you. I loved your mother with everything in me. When I lost her, I felt myself die and I blamed you. I was wrong. I love you, son. Thank you for all that you've done for me, including cleaning up my mistakes. If I could do things again, I would do them much differently. I am so proud of the man you have become. The best thing you've done is allow Nash into your life. She loves you like your mother loved me. Don't ever take that for granted son. Keep her heart close and she will heal yours. I love you. Please find forgiveness.

. . .

Dad

I STARE at the book for a few minutes, as if it might start talking to me in my father's voice. Then I stand and let it drop to the floor. Because of my pride, and selfishness, I've lost them both.

CHAPTER TWENTY THREE

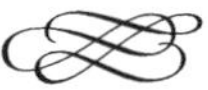

NASH

When I first got back home I cried for days. Momma and daddy had to coax me out of my room. I felt sick all the time. Slowly as the weeks passed, I got myself back together and started working at the local doctor's office. I enrolled in school to get my master's degree so that I could become a nurse practitioner. Being busy helped me to miss August a little less.

When it was quiet, I wondered what he was doing. I googled him, and he was in the headlines a lot for a while. He looked bone tired in most of his pictures. He was somehow able to save his company, but in none of his pictures did he ever have a smile on his face. Even his eyes seemed darker.

Anna came to visit one weekend and took me out

to a local bar for line dancing. None of the guys were the least bit appealing to me.

"Have a beer. That always cheers you up." Anna slides a cold draft in front of me.

I place the glass to my lips, but the familiar smell nauseates me. I try to fight it for a minute, but I start sweating. I get off the barstool and head for the front door. I make it outside just in time to puke off the bar's little front porch.

"Whoa! Are you okay?" Anna asks as she holds my hair away from my face.

"I guess I'm still not over this stomach bug." I wipe my lips with the back of my hand.

"Nash, sweetie. When was the last time you had a visit from your monthly friend?"

The blood drains from my face. I suddenly feel faint. Anna helps me sit on the ground.

"So, I take it, it's been a while?" She fans my face.

"I can't be. I was on the pill."

"You were also sick and on some antibiotics, right? Did you and August have sex while you were on the medication?"

I remember that morning very well. August had taken such good care of me that I wanted to thank him. I feel queasy again. I cover my mouth.

"Breathe. Just breathe through it." Anna helps me off the ground.

"I don't want to be pregnant." Tears sting my eyes. "I can't be pregnant."

"Let's go to your office and get a pregnancy test so we know for sure. No use panicking over nothing."

* * *

I PEE ON THE STICK, but I can't look at it. The last thing I need is to be pregnant.

"Let me see." Anna rushes into the bathroom. Her face has no expression as she stares at the plastic tubing.

"Well?" I finally ask.

She turns it so that I can see it. Blue marks. Positive. I start to cry and Anna wraps her arms around me.

"What am I going to do? I don't want to raise a baby by myself and I can't tell August."

"You know as well as I do, that you have two choices. I can't decide for you, but I'll support whatever you decide."

"I can't keep it. I sent him his father's journal. If anything should've made him contact me, I thought that would. He obviously doesn't want to have anything to do with me."

"You don't know that for sure. Did you two ever talk about having kids?"

"No. It never came up. It seems like if he never talked about it, he didn't want them."

"That's a pretty big assumption."

"I need some time to think. I need to make a doctor's appointment. I need to decide if I'm going to tell my parents. I should be about three months along. If I'm going to do something about this, I need to do it soon."

Anna squeezes my hand. "That's all very practical Nash. But what about how you feel?"

I shake my head. I can't answer that question because I don't know.

* * *

A MONTH LATER, and I'm finally feeling like myself again. I'm happy with my decision. I moved out of my mom and dads' place, and I bought myself a cute little house on the edge of town. A stream runs through the property. A fire pit off the back porch makes pleasant, cool Tennessee nights. I sit out here most evenings and watch the fireflies. The house is simple, and it's all I need. I decorate everything in blue and white. Colors that calm me. I even spent a little money on some artwork from a local artisan's gallery. My favorite piece is a painting of two zebras. I love the contrast of black and white against the soft blue walls. I also hung the portrait mother had taken of me when I was sixteen. It's above the fireplace. In the photo, I'm sitting on a half red barn door, and I'm wearing a white dress and my cowboy boots. It reminds me of carefree days that seem so long ago.

I'm sipping a glass of lemonade when Anna pulls up. She's been visiting her own parents, and it's good to have her around." Are you ready to climb?" she asks me.

"I haven't been climbing since my last trip with August." I haven't said his name in a while.

"It's going to be great. I have everything packed and ready to go. Are you sure you wouldn't rather fly to Utah?"

"I'm positive. A road trip will be fun."

"Are you really sure that you are up to it?" She rubs my belly.

"I'm positive. If I wait too much longer this little girl of mine will be in the way."

"How did your mom and dad take the news?"

"They're so excited to have a granddaughter, but they worry so much about me." I sip my drink.

"Still not called August?" She joins me with a drink.

"I don't think a baby would be good news for August. It's been almost two months since I sent him the journal and I haven't heard a word."

"Do you miss him?"

I answer honestly." I wish every day that things could have worked out. I love him. That's why I decided to keep this little girl." I rub my tummy." She's part of him. I don't want to forget how much I loved her daddy."

"You're a better woman than me. I'd want to kill the bastard." .

"Don't say that. I know August loved me and I don't regret a minute of our time together. Not even the fighting. I sure miss the sex, though. Especially with my hormones raging."

Anna chokes on her lemonade, laughing." You never talk about sex."

"I don't think it'll ever be the same with anyone else. The man sure knew what he was doing."

"You're right. Your hormones have taken over."

* * *

We head out early the next morning. We sing at the top of our lungs and let our hair fly in the wind. I haven't laughed so hard in a long time. We make it into our hotel room just after midnight and we both fall fast asleep.

We are at Zion by seven in the morning, strapped up and ready to go. I have to loosen my belt to make room for my growing belly. I have just a small bump. Just enough that everyone knows I'm pregnant. I'm glad. I wasn't crazy about the in-between time where I just felt fat. I wanted to wear a tee shirt that said: "I'm not fat—I'm pregnant!" Now that the bump has arrived, I don't need to broadcast it.

This is the exact same spot that August and I climbed. I am happy at the memory." This is where your daddy and I climbed." I rest a hand on my belly. I've just started to feel those first fluttery movements in the past few days. I feel a tickle now. I think my little girl heard me.

CHAPTER TWENTY FOUR

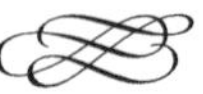

AUGUST

Sam and I are at the base of the mountain, ready for the last climb. It's the last climb because I'm moving. It's time for me to get on with my life. He's about to go off to college. Claire is seeing a nice man and talking about getting married. I've sold the company to Italian investors, and my Utah house is on the market. Stella was terrified at first, but I promised her, no matter where I am, she'll have a job with me. I'm ready for the *next* chapter, but I have to make this last climb with Sam. Sam, who now walks unassisted all the time, and doesn't need the braces I had made for him. It's amazing to me what a year can do to a man's life.

We are at the base of the mountain by nine in the morning. Sam still moves a little slow. It's just the two of us this time. Sam refuses any extra help. He's walking great, but I have to admit it scares me a little. I make him climb in front of me and I refuse to take my eyes off him.

It takes us three and a half hours to reach the top. We're both covered in sweat and our bodies are aching. I pour some water over my head. I'm sprawled out on a rock when a familiar voice catches my attention. I'll never mistake that voice. I look around. Her back is to me, but I know it's her. She is talking to Anna.

The two of them are plotting their climb down the rock wall. I stand up and Anna sees me. She whispers to Nash, and she turns her head in my direction. Her eyes widen, and I'm pretty sure her face pales. It's hard to tell since she's flushed from the effort of the climb. She's beautiful, as always. I gulp more water. My mouth is dry, and I don't want to be tongue-tied this time. I run my hands through my drenched hair. I walk toward them. Nash is holding a coiled rope in front of her. Anna is scowling at me, but Nash has a sweet smile on her face.

"Hi,"I say as I reach her.

"What do you want?" Anna snaps.

"Anna, please," Nash says. Anna rolls her eyes and walks away.

"Hi." She holds up one hand, shielding her eyes from the sun.

"You look good."

"Are you here with Sam?"

"Yea, it's his first climb without his braces. He did great." I look her up and down.

"How are you?"

"I'm good. I was going to be in Nashville this week and I was going to look you up."

"Oh, were you now?"

I run my hand down her arm and that same electrical feeling is still there." I've missed you, Nash. I wanted to see if we could talk. I've made a few changes in my life that I think you would like."

She doesn't say anything.

"I know it's taken me some time to work my shit out, but please give me a chance."

She closes her eyes. "There's something you need to know." She unlatches her vest.

"You're pregnant." I can't believe it.

"I don't need anything from you. I just thought you should know before you said anything else."

I step close and put my hand on her belly." You

may not need me Nash, but I need you. And this little one." I kiss her forehead.

"It's not that simple August. You and I didn't work...."

I stop her by placing my finger on her lips." We can work if you will just hear me out, but this is not the time nor the place to talk about it. Can I call you tonight?"

"I don't know. This is so out of the blue."

"It's fate, don't you think? What are the chances of us being on this mountain at the same time and day?"

"I think you're stalking her again," says Anna.

"I promise this was a pure coincidence."

"We really need to head down the mountain, Nash." Anna's hands are on her hips.

"Oh my god. Nash, is that really you?" Sam appears out of nowhere and embraces Nash.

"Look at you, doing this all on your own." She hugs him back.

"Hi, Anna." Sam smiles at her.

"I had no idea," says Anna. "You've come a long way since the last time I saw you."

"Thanks to August."

"This is all you, Sam." I put my hand on his shoulder. Anna's face softens a little.

"Anna is right. We do need to start heading down." Nash adjusts her vest and picks up the rope.

"I'll call you if that's okay." I'm silently pleading with her. Anna rolls her eyes and tugs Nash away.

Sam leans into me." Dude, is she pregnant?"

"Can we talk about this later?"

"August is going to be a daddy. Your life really is about to change."

* * *

WE STAY A LITTLE LONGER, but I keep looking over the edge to keep an eye on Nash. Her climbing skills are phenomenal as always, but I can't help but be concerned.

As Sam and I descend climb, my mind is only on her. I've never really given much thought to having children, but I am genuinely excited.

A baby.

A baby with Nash.

Nash and I are going to have a baby.

I'm going to have a son or a daughter, with Nash.

My head is spinning and my heart is full. I'll do everything in my power to win her back.

CHAPTER TWENTY FIVE

NASH

"Are you really considering giving him another chance?"

Anna has been on a rant from the moment we got into the car.

"What's so wrong with me hearing him out? You're the one who thought I should tell him when we found out about this."

"I know. But it's been forever, and you haven't heard from him. What an asshole."

"I wasn't innocent. I knew there was a big chance that we would never be able to work out our differences. But, I fell for him hard and I was willing to give it a chance."

"You gave it a chance. You gave it a bunch of

chances. You were on an emotional roller coaster with him. That can't be good for the baby."

"I know you're right, but I still love him and I would love for this little girl to have a daddy."

"She can have a daddy without you being involved with him."

I cover my face with my hands. How did this all turn out this way? It's like a bad dream, and the baby is the only happy part of the vision. Anna pulls over on the side of the Interstate.

"I want you to be happy," she says." If you really think that August is the one that will make you happy, then I'll support you. But know this, if he hurts you again, I'll go to jail." She pats my hand and I laugh.

"You'd kill him wouldn't you?"

"Don't test me."

I SLEEP the rest of the ride back to the hotel. This little one makes me exhausted.

My back hurts, and I just want to put my feet up. "I'm going to get us something to eat while you rest." Anna heads out the door.

I wash my face and put on a fuzzy robe. The

silence is relaxing. I'm grateful to Anna for caring so much, but I need a break. I don't get much of one because my phone rings. It vibrates against the bathroom counter. August's face appears. I love this picture of him. I snapped it the night we went bowling with Sam and Claire. He looks so carefree and young.

"Hello," I say.

"Hey beautiful, I was afraid you weren't going to answer."

"Tell her congratulations." Sam is yelling in the background.

"I'm sorry. I couldn't wait until I got back to call you." He whispers.

"It's okay. Tell Sam thank you."

"When are you going to be back in Tennessee?"

"I'll be back by tomorrow night."

"Can I come see you?"

"Yes." I take a deep breath. I'm really going to let him back in. "I don't live with my parents anymore.... wait, do you already know where I live?"

"No, I gave up stalking you."

"Wow, you really have changed. I'll text you my address."

"Goodnight, Nash."

"Goodnight, August."

* * *

"If I keep eating like this I'm going to be huge." I say as I stuff my face with Pizza."

"You're eating for two now. Besides, I think you burned enough calories today." Anna slurps her Coke.

"He called me already."

"He moves quickly. When are you going to see him?"

"Tomorrow night."

She frowns." So soon? You two jumped into this crazy relationship so quickly last time. You barely had the chance to get to know one another."

"You're right we did, but I was just so drawn to him. I still am. I get butterflies when I'm around him."

"Are you sure that's not waves of nausea?"

"You are awful. I don't know why we are even friends."

But we laugh anyway. I know exactly why we're friends. Because no one makes me laugh when I'm sad like Anna. I hope I do the same for her.

The ride home from Utah was long, and I'm anxious about seeing August. I drag my bags through my front door, but Anna doesn't have hers.

"Aren't you staying here tonight?" I ask.

"No way, no how. I'm going to crash at your parents' house. You and August need some time alone."

She's right, but I can't help but be a little nervous about being alone with him. I know how he makes my body react. My hormones are raging, and I need to focus on keeping my hands off of him. He should be here in about an hour. I take a quick shower and put on a pair of shorts and a t-shirt.

Before I even have my hair blown out, I hear a knock on the door. I run a brush through it and trot to the door with my heart racing. I open it, and there is August with a bunch of flowers. He's wearing jeans and his red Ford t-shirt.

"These are beautiful. Thank you." I take the flowers from him and place them on the table as he saunters into my house. I watch him out of the corner of my eye. He is sexy as sin.

"Your hair is still wet. Did I come too early?" He twirls a small section of my hair.

"No, I was running behind. You're right on time." I motion for him to sit on the couch.

"I like your place. It fits you." He says looking around.

"It's perfect for the two of us,"I say as I rub my little baby bump.

"How far along are you?"

"Four and a half months."

"Is there anything you need?"

"No." *I need you.* That's what I want to tell him.

He is quiet for a moment.

"I sold my company."

I'm glad I'm sitting down. I would've fallen over from shock." You did what?"

He gets up and starts pacing." I thought a lot about the things you said to me. My business has never really made me happy. It was for survival. I don't want to just survive anymore. I want to be happy. Everything is out in the open now. No more secrets. I have even sold my house in Utah." He stops and faces me.

"You sold your house?" I can't seem to do anything but parrot what he is saying.

"Yes. And tomorrow I want to take you by our new house."

"Wait. I have a house. You can't just come in here and take control again. We haven't spoken in months, and here you come, declaring we have a new home. It doesn't work that way. We have things we need to work out. And your control issue is one of them."

He kneels down in front of me." Let me start over." He takes my hands in his." I love you. I've never needed or wanted someone so bad in my life. I was an ass to ever let you go. I bought a house here in Nashville, and after I've persuaded you that I'm a changed man, I would love for you and this little one to live with me and make our house a home. I was coming back for you before I knew anything about this baby. He or she is an added bonus. I'll work on my control issues, but I've given everything else up for you. I even traded in my Jaguar for a pickup truck."

"She."

He smiles so big." It's a girl?"

"Yes. A girl."

He takes me in his arms and his mouth consumes me. God, I've missed this. The taste of him overwhelms my senses, but I pull back from him.

"We can't do this." I'm breathless.

"You mean we can't be together? Or I can't make love to you?" He is frowning.

"I want us to go slower this time. So there will be no sex until we get some things sorted out."

"Now that I've kissed, you I don't think I can do that." His mouth is on my neck.

"I'm serious. I want us to date and get to know one another first."

"I know every inch of you." He hisses in my ear.

I pull his head back to look at him." I'm serious, August. No sex."

"For how long?" He is pouting and it is positively *adorable.*

"Until our wedding night."

"So, we're getting married tomorrow?"

"No. We're not getting married until I know that I can trust you. Until we are both able to make some compromises."

"I'm done compromising. I'll give you and this little girl whatever you want." He lays his head on my belly and kisses it.

He's not going to make this very easy. My damn fingers are already itching to touch him.

"Can I stay here tonight?"

"You can stay in the guest room. You'll not sneak in my room in the middle of the night."

"What if I promise to be a complete gentleman and just hold you and our daughter?"

"Do you think you can do that?"

"Do you still have your Hello Kitty nightshirt?"

I look at him confused." Yes."

"Wear it and then I can do it."

"I knew you hated that shirt." I swat his chest.

He lets me get changed before he crawls into bed. He draws me to him and places his hand protectively on my belly. He whispers in my ear." I love you and this little girl. I'll prove to you that I'm the man you need." He kisses the top of my head and tucks me into him further. I choose to ignore the erection I can feel poking me in the back. This is definitely not going to be easy.

I miss waking up to his handsome face. He's sound asleep sprawled out in his shorts. No covers. I want to touch him so badly, but I don't dare, so I admire his body. I feel like a peeping tom. His chest is so defined, and his arms are muscular from climbing. I like the stubble of beard on his face. There is not much that I don't love about him. I hope our baby has his complexion and dark hair with my blue eyes. She will be beautiful. August may never let her leave the house.

I can't help myself. I softly place my hand on his abdomen. He stirs and says my name but doesn't wake. I trace my fingers down his goody trail and his cock grows firmer. My eyes get big watching him.

"Did we get married last night? I don't remember it." He's teasing me, so I remove my hand.

"I'm not complaining," he says. "You can wake me anytime with your hands on my body." He rolls on his side to face me. His head is propped on his hand.

"Sorry," I say. "I just wanted to make sure you were real."

He looks at his cock and then back at me." I'm real alright." He has a mischievous smile.

I pull the sheet up and bite at it." This is going to be really hard."

"Umm...I think it is already hard." He laughs and pushes toward me.

"Stop. You're not helping." I laugh at him. I hop out of bed." I need a cold shower."

"Oh, can I watch?" He is all smiles. I like him this way. This is the August I love. The silly, sexy, sweet August.

"Why don't you get up and make us some coffee?"

I come out of the shower and I can smell bacon cooking. I'm terrified at the thought of August cooking, so I quickly dress. He might burn the house down.

"What are you doing?" I ask.

He looks at the pan and then looks back at me." I thought I was cooking bacon?"

"Have you ever cooked bacon before?" I say as I walk up beside him.

"I read the instructions. I've watched Stella do it." He says smugly." Now go sit down and let me finish." He shoos me out with the spatula.

I sit down at the small table in the kitchen and watch him. He's so animated. He looks at his phone when he's mixing the eggs. I walk up behind him and grab it." You're texting Stella?"

"I need all the help I can get to impress you. Now give me back my phone before whatever I'm mixing becomes inedible."

I stand on my tippy toes and kiss his nose." You're so adorable.

He points at his shirt. There are cows and pigs cavorting all over it. It's ridiculous, and I think of how for the first few months I knew him, I couldn't even get him to wear a Ford t-shirt. Now here he is, covered in farm animals and splattered grease.

"Only for you baby," he says. "Only for you."

* * *

He really did buy a pickup truck. Not your typical beat up pickup truck. It's dark gray and loaded with everything imaginable. We're both quiet as he drives. I think maybe he's nervous about showing me the house. He drives through a covered bridge and up the side of a mountain and stops in front of a log cabin home. The land is beautiful. Part of it's mountainous, and part is green pasture. A river runs through the land.

"This is beautiful." He takes my hand and leads me to the front porch. I'm in awe when he opens the door. It's simply decorated with nice leather furniture. The ceilings are high and there is a mezzanine overlooking the living room. The kitchen opens up the back of the house. A farm style table takes up one entire corner of the room. He walks me up the polished wooden staircase to a beautiful open master bedroom. A balcony overlooks the property, and the bathroom is massive. The shower walls are built with blocks. A fireplace separates the bedroom from the bathroom.

He breaks the silence." There are two more

bedrooms downstairs. One of them would make a great nursery. Stella and her husband will stay in the other one until I have their cabin built out back."

I walk up close to him." You really sold your company and your house and purchased this house before you even knew how I would react?"

"You said it yourself. I needed a change. You asked me, *what's next August?*" He looks around the room." This is what's *next.* I love you. I was determined to win you back."

"I love that you've done all this for me. But, is this what is going to make you happy? You're a city boy at heart. Can you live like this?"

"My heart belongs to you and our daughter, nothing else matters to me anymore. I've had all the finer things in life, I've traveled to beautiful places, but none of it means anything to me without you. We still have more money than we'll ever spend and we can have a great life together, but I want that life with you. If that means learning how to be a country boy then so be it."

"It doesn't all have to be about me August, we just need to compromise."

"Don't worry. I'll still be controlling and you'll want for nothing."

I step up and kiss him on the cheek." I like some of your controlling ways."

"Good, because I like when you let me control you." Our kiss heats up.

I feel the baby kick. Those kicks are getting stronger. I break our kiss and place his hand on my belly." Feel this."

"It feels like a flutter."

"That's your daughter kicking me."

He gets on his knees and kisses my belly. "I love you little one. I promise I'll take good care of you and your mommy if she'll let me."

I run my hands through his hair. He reaches into his pocket and pulls out a small box. He opens it and there's a simple silver ring with a square diamond in the middle." Will you marry me, Nash?"

My eyes begin to water. Two days ago I thought I'd lost this beautiful man forever, and now here he is in front of me asking me to be his wife. There's only one possible answer for him.

"Yes, August, I'll marry you." He places the ring on my finger and I pull him up to me. We kiss deeply.

"Do you think we could do it soon because I don't know how much longer I can keep my hands off of you," he says between kisses.

"We can find the justice of the peace today."

He picks me up and twirls me around the room.

"August, put me down, you're making me dizzy. I still get queasy pretty easily."

"I love you, Nash."

"I love you, too. But I need two more promises from you."

"I'm afraid to ask."

"One. I want you to at least try a pair of cowboy boots because I'd love to peel them off of you like you do me."

"Deal."

"Two. I want to name our little girl Sara."

I see tears form in his deep brown eyes. He kisses me again. He rubs my belly." Sara Rylan," he whispers it, and it sounds just right.

Please consider leaving a review

Get the next book

This August FREE

ABOUT THE AUTHOR

Kelly Moore writes so the characters inside her head can come to life. She writes sexy, steamy, suspenseful romance stories, laced with a touch of humor.

Her true addictions include traveling, exploring old books stores for treasures, laughing with friends and family, eating mint Oreo ice cream, and spoiling her grandchildren rotten.

She is a critical care nurse by day and an author by night. Writing settles her mind and spirit, plus she gets to spend her days in her pajamas.

ALSO BY KELLY MOORE

Whiskey River Road Series - Available on Audible

Coming Home, Book 1

Stolen Hearts, Book 2

Three Words, Book 3

Kentucky Rain, Book 4

Wild Ride, Book 5

Magnolia Mill, Book 6

Rough Road, Book 7

Lucky Man, Book 8 Aug 12 2021 (PreOrder)

Simple Man Late 2021

The Broken Pieces Series in order

Broken Pieces

Pieced Together

Piece by Piece

Pieces of Gray

Syn's Broken Journey

Broken Pieces Box set Books 1-3

August Series in Order

Next August

This August

Seeing Sam

The Hitman Series- Previously Taking Down Brooklyn/The DC Seres

Stand By Me - On Audible as Deadly Cures

Stay With Me On Audible as Dangerous Captive

Hold Onto Me

Epic Love Stories Series can be read in any order

Say You Won't Let Go. Audiobook version

Fading Into Nothing Audiobook version

Life Goes On. Audiobook version

Gypsy Audiobook version

Jameson Wilde Audiobook version

Rescue Missions Series can be read in any order

Imperfect. On Audible

Blind Revenge

Fated Lives Series

Rebel's Retribution Books 1-4. Audible

Theo's Retaliation Books 5-7. Audible

Thorn's Redemption Audible

Fallon's Revenge Book 11 Audible

The Crazy Rich Davenports Season One in order of reading

The Davenports On Audible

Lucy

Yaya

Ford

Gemma

Daisy

The Wedding

Halloween Party

Bang Bang

Coffee Tea or Me